Books by James Litherland

The Slowpocalypse Series

Certain Hypothetical
Threat Multiplication
Compromised Inside

The Watchbearers Series

Millennium Crash
Centenary Separation
Uncertain Murder

The Miraibanashi Series

Whispers of the Dead

For more information, please visit
www.OutpostStories.com

CENTENARY SEPARATION

DEDICATION

To God be the Glory

(and all criticism should go to the author.)

CENTENARY SEPARATION

James Litherland

Outpost Stories

Disclaimer: As should be obvious, this book is a complete work of fiction. Any resemblance to real persons, places or things is entirely coincidental.

Copyright © 2014 James Litherland
All rights reserved.
ISBN: 0692265341
ISBN-13: 978-0692265345

Cover design by James Litherland

The Watchbearers

Ten researchers from the far future came to the summer of the year 2000, each wearing their own time-travel device disguised as a watch. Those devices do not all have the same capabilities. Three of those people have died (Harold, Kirin, and Professor John) with their watches having passed to other hands.

MATT WALKER—native of 2000 and graduate student of physics. He's now in possession of the professor's master time-travel device—theoretically capable of unlimited travel through time and space, it was damaged in the accident that killed the professor. Supposedly it's been fixed.

PAGE—a research team leader and mathematician who came to study the dating customs of the twentieth century, her 'leader' device can only travel up to three years in one trip. It also grants her access to funds from a trust which was established to finance their research.

ANYA—a former nurse turned historian, and senior team leader, she was the closest to the late professor and assumed responsibility for the research expedition as a whole. For what that was worth.

SAM—a former research assistant who has Harold's leader device. She became a team leader by default, following the deaths of Harold and Kirin (and does not appear in this story.)

VERITY—another native of 2000, she's ended up in possession of Samantha's old 'helper' device, which is only capable of time travel when it's within range of another device that's being used to travel through time.

TURNER—technically one of Anya's assistants, he'd been functioning as Page's helper. A former preacher, now he's Verity's (brand new) husband.

NYE—also a research assistant of Anya's, supposedly, she'd specialized in the study of the ruins of New York City before coming to the past to study the living city. (And she's a bit different.)

TATE—technically one of Page's assistants, he's the only one who's been functioning as Anya's helper.

BAILEY—another assistant assigned to Page, they'd been separated, and now he follows Sam. (And like her, he doesn't appear in this story.)

???—Kirin's 'helper' device disappeared, and no one knows who has it now. Like every device, it is capable (purportedly) of tracking the physical location of the other devices.

Contents

Prologue: All Alone	1
Chapter 1: Worst Honeymoon Ever	11
Chapter 2: In the Wilderness	25
Chapter 3: A Walk in the Park	33
Chapter 4: A Day Late	48
Chapter 5: Nye and the FBI	61
Chapter 6: *Though I Know I Shouldn't*	76
Chapter 7: No One There	92
Chapter 8: Stranger in a Strange Land	109
Chapter 9: Along for the Ride	118
Chapter 10: Parade Rout(e)	133
Chapter 11: Nye on the Street	145
Chapter 12: *I Have to Do Something*	154
Chapter 13: Anticipating Events	169
Chapter 14: The Good Samaritans	181
Chapter 15: Out of the Frying Pan	191
Chapter 16: Playing with Fire	204
Chapter 17: Nye in the Soup	216
Chapter 18: *I Can't Help Myself*	226

Chapter 19: An Inside Job	236
Chapter 20: Providence	248
Chapter 21: An Experiment in Hope	256
Chapter 22: Unscheduled Appointments	273
Chapter 23: Nye at the Ngaio	284
Chapter 24: Expecting	295
Epilogue: A New Life	306

Prologue
All Alone

September 8th, 2002 Chickadee County, NY

ANYA tried to think as she gazed out the window of their hired car as it sailed along the interstate in the dark—she didn't have a plan, yet, but if she were going to accomplish the impossible, she should be well prepared. Theoretically, it simply couldn't be done. But Anya was none too strong on time-travel theory anyway. She was a practical woman, and looking at the problem from her perspective, changing history would be difficult. Even though it was her own personal history, and she knew well enough what needed to be altered.

They had left New York City far behind, and all Anya saw out the window were the red tail-lights of

Prologue

other vehicles heading north and the bright spots of white speeding past that were people headed in the other direction. Anya would soon be home—not her real home, far in the future, but the house just outside the town of Little Piece in Chickadee County, in this early part of the third millennium.

Her attention was drawn to Nye, who was shifting in her seat and checking her watch. Nye looked up at Anya. "It's ten thirty-five. The others ought to be long gone—if it actually worked."

Anya sighed. Sitting quietly next to her with his round red face and bald pate, Tate would've left her to her thoughts. He knew visiting the city made her mindful of tragedy—between memories of the professor's accident and 9/11 she didn't know why she kept putting herself through it. But if she was going to do what she was contemplating, she'd have to return to the city a few more times. She'd just have to be strong.

But nothing could keep Nye silent for long. Anya gave in and checked her leader watch, scrolling to the locator screen where she saw two white blips in the center, representing Tate and Nye. And nothing else. "There's no red bar to indicate any other Travel devices, in any direction. They've all left the present. Page and Turner aren't with us anymore." Or Matt or Verity, but they were natives of this age, and that was different.

Anya had tried to reunite the time-travelers, after they'd all been scattered and separated on their initial arrival in the past, but she'd found only a few of her fellow researchers. And now she'd lost half of those she'd gathered back together. The entire expedition had fallen apart from the start and now the pieces were falling through her fingers as everyone went their own way.

She'd hoped that young Matt, however brilliant he might be for a contemporary, would be unable to fix the professor's master Travel device, which had been smashed in the accident.

Nye nodded. "So it did work, at least partially. If it worked correctly, then they're now ten years in the future."

Anya smiled. It wasn't often that she got to correct Nye. "They were aiming for June first, twenty twelve. Not *quite* ten years." And tomorrow morning Anya would be taking these two to next summer. "I suppose as soon as we're in two thousand three, you'll be heading back into the city to continue your research?"

The girl stared back with that blank expression on her face, her eyes wide behind those giant glasses of hers. "Of course. What else would I be doing?"

"Well, I'm not going to be staying in the city all summer with you, so there'll be no one to supervise you and your work."

Prologue

"Page was always too absorbed in *her* research to pay any attention to what I was doing—not that I acknowledge that I need any supervision—and Turner was too absorbed in Verity. I managed."

Anya shook her head. "But at least Page and the rest were right there to help, if you had gotten yourself into trouble. Next summer no one will be there to come to your aid." Anya paused and considered. "Although I *will* come and check up on you now and then." That would give her an excuse to go into the city to make preparations.

Once they'd arrived in two thousand three, Anya would still have weeks to plan before she passed the three-year limit, to be able to make the journey in one trip. After that she could still try, but multiple trips would only add unnecessary complications and create more room for error—not the best notion when she had no idea what the consequences would be if she were to *succeed* in changing the past. She didn't like to think what might happen if she failed to save the professor.

All her memories of John were in the future except for that one—the heart-breaking moment when his life had been cut short just at what should have been the beginning of his greatest work, the culmination of decades of effort. They'd all arrived in the summer of the year two thousand, but the professor had materialized in the middle of a busy street. And

Anya hadn't been able to *do* anything, just watch in horror as a black SUV struck and killed him.

She glanced over at Tate. "It's certainly been an uneventful summer. For a change."

"That's a good thing, isn't it?"

She smiled at him. "Well, we definitely needed the rest." After all the adventures they'd had on first arriving in the past, then coping with so many unexpected difficulties, there'd been the frisson of living in the middle of history. And then 9/11.

Tate must've been thinking of the aftermath of that attack. "You pushed yourself too hard, Leader. Maybe it would've been better if you had not volunteered at all."

Anya shook her head. "I couldn't help as much as I wanted, but I had to do what I could." Not being a nurse anymore, that hadn't been much more than handing out water bottles and helping clean up debris and giving people a shoulder to cry on.

"I would've thought you'd seen enough horrors already for one lifetime. With what you had to work in the middle of, back in the future."

Indeed, that was why she'd given up nursing to become a historian. Then she'd ended up as part of the professor's research expedition into the past, to only encounter more tragedy.

"Maybe we shouldn't have come into the city to celebrate. It's almost the one year anniversary, and

Prologue

the memory remains raw." Even more so for them, as it had only been four months ago.

Tate shook his head. "That's why we should rejoice all the more when we have reason. And I think getting those two young people properly hitched before they got into trouble was a good cause for celebration."

"Turner used to be a preacher, so he would have made that relationship right before it went too far—anyway, we celebrated that enough at the reception yesterday." Anya smiled at the memory. "The ceremony was good, even if it was rather small. And at least Mr. Hollingsworth was able to attend."

Nye interjected. "He's our lawyer, and you pay him enough that he should show up when you want him. Anyway, it was a Saturday. He probably didn't have any work to do."

"He's earned every penny we paid him. He got me out of jail, and since he got you out of that mental hospital, I'd have hoped you'd be grateful."

"He was just doing his job. Besides, I was gathering some interesting information in there. They'd have had to let me out before long anyway."

Anya sniffed. "Only if you could convince them you weren't crazy. And Mr. Hollingsworth came because he likes us—he stayed for the reception, didn't he?" And after that smorgasbord, they'd all gone to the house in Chickadee for a fabulous feast for dinner. Except for the newlyweds, who'd been left behind at their hotel suite. Anya turned to Tate. "We celebrated Turner and Verity's tying the knot *more* than enough yesterday." They'd stuffed themselves with Italian tonight, to the point where Anya wasn't sure she'd be able to get out of the car.

Tate shook his head. "So what do we say tonight was for?"

As if Anya needed an excuse to pig out. "Besides needing to get well away from the others while they Traveled, so we wouldn't be dragged along? We had the end of the summer to celebrate." They certainly weren't rejoicing at being left behind.

"And next summer to look forward to."

"Just the two of us? You heard Nye say she'll be headed straight back to the city. With the rest gone on to the future, that means you and me on our own for the next nine summers. I appreciate your companionship, Tate, but I can't say I'm exactly looking forward to not having the others around."

"That's just what *this* summer was. The two of us at the house in Chickadee, and the rest spending all their time in the city. What's different now?"

If he didn't understand it, Anya couldn't explain —there was a big difference between the others being an hour's drive away in the city and ten years in the future. Unreachable. Except for Nye of course, but that girl was inaccessible in another way.

Prologue

The feel of the car slowing down made her look out the window again, but it was too dark to see—in the country, the night was much blacker. She could feel the car turn off the paved road though, and start trundling down the dirt lane that led to their house. Soon she saw the porch light glaring.

The car eased to a halt. The driver came around and opened the door for her, and Anya climbed out with a weary sigh. Then she took a deep breath and smiled at him. "Thank you, Ralph. We won't need you again until next summer." And she slipped him his usual twenty-dollar tip.

Tate exited on the other side and walked around to stand next to her as she stopped and stared at the house—while Nye bounded past them to the porch. Light seeped from cracks in the living room curtains but the rest was dark. Anya gave Ralph a brief wave as he turned the car around, then waited for the taillights to recede before looking back at Tate.

"It's empty. They're gone." *How can an empty house be home?*

"Maybe. But instead of ten years in the future, they might be waiting for us in three years' time, or even in next summer."

Anya shook her head. "Or they could be a hundred years in the future or the past for all we know, or have any way of finding out. I never should've let them go."

Though Page refused to accept that she was Anya's responsibility, and Matt never really had been, Anya would always consider them her charges, and Turner too, whatever compromise she'd agreed upon—Verity as well, now they were married. But they had all gone their own way, and Anya felt helpless to keep them from drifting out of her care—she should never have gotten out of the habit of giving orders. They wouldn't even listen to her advice anymore.

Tate nodded. "But I don't think we should worry about them. We have our own work to do, which is plenty enough even if we aren't going to be supervising Nye in the city. And there's taking care of the house and the garden. You enjoy that."

Anya smiled at him. "I know we'll keep busy—and Nye can always call us for help if she needs it." Or Mr. Hollingsworth, and learn to appreciate him more. "But the others can't call for help."

Tate watched Nye pacing back and forth across the porch. "It will be peaceful."

"And bicycling around the neighborhood to talk to people—it will help us work off all this food we've been eating."

She could start exercising by climbing those few shallow steps up onto the porch. Tate lumbered up after her. She unlocked the front door, and Nye ran into the narrow hall and up the stairs. Anya walked into the house at a more sedate pace.

Prologue

Turning on more lights only made the place feel even emptier. Peaceful it might be, but the idea of spending one summer after another doing the same routine research—Anya knew she would not be content with that. But starting tomorrow with a hearty breakfast would help.

It might be different to truly take the slow path and live like a native, become a part of the community. Maybe then she could find something more to do than just the research, something that would really satisfy her—but before she could consider a step like that, she had to at least try to go back and save the professor. Though she knew it was reckless.

She knew she shouldn't even be thinking about it—maybe she would come to her senses and give up the idea altogether, but she doubted it. She was going to break the rules and *not* leave her past alone.

Chapter 1

Worst Honeymoon Ever

September 8th, 2012 The Berkshires

VERITY had kept her eyes closed for the journey, not wanting to watch reality disappear around her—what had vanished were Turner's arms holding her. She'd heard them talk about this phenomenon, being physically separated as they traveled. But they'd assured her that couldn't happen while her husband held her tight. So much for their promises.

She kept her eyes shut as she felt tears begin to well up behind her eyelids. *What a great start to my honeymoon.*

From Turner's sudden proposal to their whirlwind wedding and the reception, and their glorious first night together, Verity had been riding an emo-

Chapter 1

tional roller coaster for days. Then there'd been the anticipation of taking her first trip through time and starting her honeymoon properly. She'd shown better control of herself as a *teenager*. Now, *something* had certainly gone wrong, but that was no reason to lose her grip.

With her eyes still closed, Verity felt the breeze blowing against her skin and heard it rustling in the leaves of trees around her. She was likely standing in the woods behind the house in Chickadee. Probably they were searching for her even now. She knew these special watches of theirs had some function to track each other, though no one had bothered to explain exactly how that was supposed to work. Matt had just strapped the thing on her wrist and said she needed to wear it to travel with them.

Still, she wasn't going to just stand around waiting. Opening her eyes wide, Verity turned her head to take a good look at her surroundings. The night was black and moonless—as her eyes began adjusting she could just make out the dark shapes of softly swaying trees. And past them, the rising hulks of gentle peaks. *I'm not in Chickadee anymore.*

They'd explained that, since it was Matt's device being used to set the coordinates for their trip, she and Turner might appear a short distance away—so much for what *they* knew. She wondered if they had even arrived in two thousand twelve.

She recalled stories of lost hikers from the news and the advice that such people should stay put and not wander around. But that was so rescuers might find them. The only ones who'd know she was missing or would be looking for her would also be able to locate her wherever she went. Supposedly. She decided not to rely on that.

Finding her husband began with getting back to the house in Chickadee, but she didn't know how far that might be, or in what direction. And she had no way to orient herself. All she could see was pristine nature and no sign of anyone, and she had no desire to wait for sunrise to figure out which way was east, when that wouldn't tell her anything useful anyway. And it was too dark to see the watch to find the time. *They* had said that they would automatically arrive at the same time of day they were leaving from—that would make it ten in the evening, if they had known what they were talking about, which Verity doubted —and dawn a long way off.

The wind moaned through the trees, and Verity pulled her light jacket more tightly around her. She needed to get in out of this bitter chill before she did anything else, and she needed to get to civilization— wherever that might be. She had to start moving.

It was too dark to walk fast, and she had to take care with each step, so she wasn't able to give much thought to her dilemma as she slowly made her way

Chapter 1

across the forest floor. At least she managed not to trip and fall.

It had been a long time since Verity had been in the real outdoors, but she had not always been a city girl. She'd grown up in Central Massachusetts, on a farm—but she'd left as soon as she could after graduating high school and tried to forget. Now she was grateful to find her background hadn't left *her*.

Insects chirping and owls hooting and the other sounds of nocturnal activity didn't disturb her and, after an initial bout of nervousness, she found it was not too tricky, walking across the uneven ground. It helped that she was dressed sensibly—due in part to the thought they might arrive outside the house, but they had also planned, she and Turner, to leave for a proper honeymoon as soon as they landed.

He hadn't told her where they were heading, or how, so she'd outfitted herself for traveling by boat, plane, or train. It would do for walking through the woods too, provided she didn't have to walk too far. Turner had wanted to surprise her for their honeymoon—well, this certainly was a shocker—and supposedly all they'd need would be waiting for them in twenty twelve, including their luggage. At least she had her purse with her, so she wasn't totally without resources, but she would've appreciated a change of clothes. With a sigh she realized she'd been a fool to allow her husband to plan everything.

Verity recalled the fall of two thousand one with a shake of her head—Turner had blithely invited her to travel with him, ahead to the following summer. He hadn't seemed to realize that just picking up and disappearing from her life, her job, for nine months with no explanation, just wasn't done. Not by her—not without his offering something more than a fun trip.

As she made her way slowly through the forest, an initial, vague sense of familiarity was growing in the back of her mind until she realized she knew the outline of those hills around her. Even then it took a while before she could dredge up the relevant memories, and then she stopped in surprise. *I'm back in the Berkshires.*

Not the Berkshires proper, where she'd headed right after graduation, but closer to the border with New York State. In the Taconics, she thought. She had gone to work in similar ski resort country to the east of here—it was there she'd worked in the tourist industry and learned a lot about how to keep things running smoothly, while also working on her associate's degree in office administration at the community college.

With that minimal accreditation in hand, she'd headed straight for New York City and miraculously landed a job as secretary to the manager of the main branch of the American International State Bank in

Chapter 1

Midtown Manhattan. She'd never looked back until now. It hadn't been all that long ago, but it felt like a lifetime.

Verity forced herself to focus. This area was not densely populated, but there ought to be a few walking trails around, and if she found one of those, that ought to lead her to people, roads, and shelter. And now that she had some idea where she was and what she was looking for, she found herself concentrating keenly on her surroundings.

With sharpened senses searching for some sign of an established path somewhere, she had no idea how much time passed before she finally found one, but it must've been hours. Then she began to enjoy herself, a bit, and make better time. She still had to go fairly slow—it was still dark, and she'd feel a fool if she tripped and sprained her ankle now. But even though a chill remained in the air, she felt refreshed by the cool breeze. *That'll be because I'm sweating so much from all the exercise.* She'd expected marriage to bring some challenges, but she hadn't imagined anything like this—even though she had known she was marrying a man from the future.

She was definitely starting to rue the change in plans that had led to this disaster. Originally, they'd only been going to take a short hop through time to the summer of two thousand three—and then take a more normal honeymoon. Or so Turner had promised. And the idea of time-traveling had been exciting enough. She should have insisted they stay with that plan, or even on the so-called slow path, which sounded quite nice.

What Verity had wanted was to spend time with her new husband—alone, not on a peculiar double date with Matt and Page, who were taking an experimental and risky journey to ten years in the future. She shouldn't have allowed herself to be persuaded. Not that resisting Turner was easy.

She let herself dwell on more pleasant thoughts until she caught her first sight of civilization, just as the first feeble shafts of sunlight were slipping over the horizon. Stopping to catch her breath, she cast her gaze past the unpaved parking area at the end of the trail to the highway and across to a proper parking lot, where a few tall light posts still shone dimly and a number of semi-trucks sat in rows. Her eyes fixed for a moment on a diner beyond.

Then she looked down at her watches. Her regular watch and the other agreed that it was six thirty in the morning—so she could likely trust the future watch's display that said it was the ninth of September, twenty twelve. They were meant to have landed on June first, but considering they had traveled ten *years*, she didn't think three months was too far off. The thing also displayed her latitude and longitude. If she'd been able to see that earlier, it would've giv-

Chapter 1

en her a general sense of her location, but she had a more specific idea of that now anyway.

Hopefully the thing would somehow inform the others where she was, but Verity didn't know how to use it to search for them—and since she looked silly wearing two watches, she took the Travel device off and stuffed it in her bag. Then she had a disturbing thought. *What if everyone else landed like we were supposed to, on the first of June?* In which case, she would've been missing for over three months now—would the others have stopped looking for her? Not Turner, surely.

Shaking her head to stop such silly speculation, Verity started walking again, across the empty road with its eerie quiet and between the giant trucks toward the diner. She needed to find her way back to Chickadee, but first she needed food.

She considered what options she would have after she ate. She didn't want to hitch a ride with one of the truck drivers she was sure to find inside, and it might be difficult to call a cab to come pick her up out here in the middle of nowhere. There should be a phone at least, and her first call should be to Turner. Unfortunately, they'd both had to give up their cell phones because they were skipping the next ten years. She would try the house in Chickadee first.

Pulling open the wide glass door, she walked into the large vestibule. On the far side sat an ancient cash register on top of a cheap plastic counter, with no one behind it. But she was reassured by the hum of human conversation from beyond. She was even happier to see an old-fashioned pay phone, hanging on the wall past a rack of raincoats.

With a sigh of relief, she dug into her purse and found some change. She slid quarters into the slot, dialed a number she'd memorized, and waited—and continued to wait as the phone kept ringing.

Next she tried their permanent suite at the hotel in Midtown. No answer there, either—but she left a message for Turner with the hotel switchboard.

Shaking her head, Verity replaced the receiver. She wouldn't give up that easy—Anya and Tate were early risers who might already be up, outside working in the garden or bicycling around the neighborhood. She'd have to find a way to make her own way there.

Before she flipped through that ratty old phone book to try to find a taxi or a car service that would come out here to pick her up though, she decided to eat breakfast and restore her energy. It was going to be a long day, and she'd already had a long and difficult night.

Verity scanned the assorted characters awaiting her as she walked into the dining room—over a dozen truckers in plaid, a harried-looking waitress in a faded blue uniform, and a person who stuck out like

Chapter 1

a sore thumb among the rest. Half-sitting on a stool at the counter, a very pregnant woman seemed to be in danger of slipping off her seat at any minute.

Seeing someone else outside their natural environment, Verity went up to the stool next to her and smiled. "Do you mind if I sit here?"

The woman smiled back and nodded before returning to an examination of the money in her billfold, or the relative lack thereof.

Verity glanced at the laminated menus littering the counter, then waved to the waitress.

Her piled-high hair trying to escape its pins, the woman walked up with a pad in her hand. "What'll you have?"

"Two Saturday Specials, please. And I'd like the eggs sunny-side up." Verity turned to the pregnant lady beside her. "And what can I get for you?"

The woman blushed but didn't demur from accepting the offer. "The same, please." She turned to the waitress. "But I'll take mine scrambled." Then she returned her billfold to her purse as the waitress scribbled the orders down and took off.

Verity and her new friend watched as the woman circled round the counter, ripped off their order slip, and handed it back to a barely seen cook in the kitchen. The waitress grabbed a half-full pot of coffee then, and came back to turn their mugs over before asking peremptorily, "Coffee?"

Verity grinned. "Yes. Please."

Her pregnant companion turned to talk as soon as the waitress had taken off again. "Thank you for that. Normally I'd balk at accepting charity, but it's rather rough at the moment. My situation."

"Yes, I can see your situation." Her grin still in place, Verity nodded across the room at the rows of padded benches lined against the windows. "Surely you'd be more comfortable sitting somewhere else. More stable too."

"I'm sure, but I'm afraid that once I wedged myself in I might not be able to get back out. I'm Karat by the way. Karat with a K."

Verity blinked. "Your parents named you after a root vegetable?"

The woman grinned. "No, silly. My father was a jeweler. So he named me after the measurement of purity for precious metals. Like gold."

"My name's Verity, so I'm in no position to cast stones."

She noticed the wedding ring on Karat's finger and decided that was a topic she'd best avoid—she had assumed the woman was a single mother when she first saw her sitting alone in a place like this. *I don't get the impression her husband's just stepped out to the men's room.* Karat had to have an interesting story to tell there, but Verity wasn't going to pry into something that wasn't her business.

Chapter 1

The waitress returned and slid four hot plates in front of them, and the women abandoned conversation to tuck into their eggs, bacon, and sausages—as well as their hash browns and toast with jam. Verity wasn't sure whether to be mortified or gratified that she managed to keep up with the pregnant woman's appetite. But after a full night of exercise, she wasn't worried about the calories.

After they'd both cleaned their plates and started on their third mugs of coffee, Karat revived their dialogue with a question. "Are you from these parts or just passing through like me?"

Verity shook her head. "Somehow I doubt that the locals eat here. I'm trying to get somewhere, but I needed fortification first. What about you?"

The woman cast an anxious look around the diner, then spoke in a low voice as if she were afraid of being overheard. "I'm on my way to New York City. Looking for someone."

Verity couldn't resist. "Your husband? So am I. Looking for my own husband, not yours. And not in New York City." Though it might come to that—the Travelers' Trust had purchased a hotel in Midtown Manhattan, and the time-travelers all had their own rooms there. She'd have to check it out if she didn't find anyone at the house in Chickadee.

Distracted by her own thoughts, she hadn't noticed Karat's eyes were welling up with tears. "My husband is dead." The woman hastily brushed tears from the corners of her eyes and tried to smile. "I'm hoping to track down an old friend of my husband's who can help me with my situation."

"I'm sorry. I didn't know."

Karat sniffed. "No reason you should've. Now, if it's not New York you're headed for, then where?"

Verity shook her head. "Chickadee County. In New York State."

"I don't think I've ever heard of it."

"It's a tiny place between Westchester and Putnam counties, between Mahopac and Katonah. I'm just not sure how I'm going to get there."

Karat managed to smile at that. "On the way to New York City. I could give you a ride, since I'll be passing not far from there anyway. We can call it a trade for my breakfast. That way neither of us has to accept any charity."

"Sounds good to me."

"On one condition."

"What's that?"

Karat blushed. "My car's a little compact hatchback, and I have a hard time fitting into the driver's seat. If you wouldn't mind driving, I could put the passenger seat back for myself."

Verity thought about how long it had been since she'd driven a car. "You'd be a good deal more comfortable. Alright. When do we leave?"

23

Chapter 1

"After I freshen up. And I'm afraid I might be a while." She sat down her cup and slid off the stool. "I shouldn't have had that third mug of coffee."

As she watched the woman waddle away toward the restroom, Verity felt a swell of hope—she would get to Chickadee sooner than she'd expected. Then she became aware that she'd been playing with the wedding band on her ring finger. It still felt strange there, but she'd get used to it after she found Turner and they had their honeymoon.

If she found him. Thinking about Karat, Verity realized that until she'd discovered what happened, she couldn't be sure her husband was still alive—she might be just as much a widow as her new companion, only not know it.

Chapter 2
In the Wilderness

September 8th, 1962 The Chihuahuan Desert

TURNER found himself standing on the sand in a stark landscape underneath a three-quarters moon, his arms empty of his new bride and no one around at all. *Thanks for giving me enough light to see my watch by.*

Then with a sigh he saw that he'd landed far off-target—both in time and space. Nineteen sixty-two put him fifty years earlier than he was supposed to be, and the latitude and longitude put him far from New York. His best estimate had him somewhere in West Texas, but his memory was fuzzy on the numbers. He hoped he hadn't landed in Mexico. It was bad enough the identification he carried would now

Chapter 2

say he'd yet to be born—if he had to cross the border into the US, he'd be in real trouble.

Scanning the lively-looking desert around him, Turner thought he was facing enough of a challenge already. It wasn't the nice, flat kind of desert. The ground undulated in an uneven pattern of little basins and dunes, with a wide array of plants littering the landscape and nocturnal animals slithering and scurrying in and around the brush. Verity would be having a rougher time of it than him, though. *Help me find her.*

Looking down at his watch again, he scrolled to the locator screen and grunted. No blip and no red bar meant no other Travelers in this time. No Verity. He didn't have any idea when or where she was, or what trials she might be facing right now, but *he* couldn't help her.

He grinned at the thought that she would want his assistance. One of the things that had attracted him to Verity was her competence—she didn't need him taking care of her. He shouldn't worry. *Lord, I'll have to leave her in Your hands.* What he should be doing was focusing on his own predicament.

With no leader device around, his own was useless for moving him anywhere—he could only travel in real time, and in one direction only, forward. The so-called slow path. As far as changing his physical location went, all he had was his two feet.

Turner was tempted to just stay there and wait, but he'd probably die if he simply sat until someone came along to rescue him. Likely he'd end up dead anyway, but he was not about to give up that easily. Aside from any other considerations, he didn't want to make Verity a widow if he could help it, especially since she wouldn't even know. He had to start moving. It was chilly, and it would surely get colder, but that would be much better than roasting during the day. *What direction should I head in?*

He could see mountains in the distance no matter which way he looked. If he was in Mexico, north or east would take him to the US, and if he was already in the States, the same would take him farther from the border. But he didn't know which way was north or east or south or west, and he couldn't know until sunrise—the stupid device didn't have a compass function. And he needed to cover as much distance as possible before dawn.

Traveling very far would be enough of an ordeal without wasting any more time—he decided to trust that he'd appeared here already facing the right way for the path he should take. He took one small step and tore his pant leg on some spiny little plant he'd not seen. He couldn't stop a sigh from escaping.

He had to find people, civilization of some sort, and soon, if he was going to survive—and he wanted to look decent when he did so. Putting one foot in

Chapter 2

front of the other, Turner trudged across the sand, trying to find the most level path forward and avoid getting scratched or catching his clothes on the various plants and bushes along the way. *Keep me from stumbling and making myself more of a mess than I already am.*

As he plodded on, dodging more of those spiny little stalks that stabbed for his shins, he wondered where and when the others were. There was no way Anya would know anything had gone wrong until or unless she ran into Page or Matt or Verity—or when two thousand twelve had rolled around and Turner hadn't shown up. That would tell the woman he still considered his leader something. Not that she'd be able to do anything about it.

The leader devices used by both Anya and Page couldn't tell them the temporal location of another Traveler. Only the professor's master Travel device supposedly did that—if it was functioning right and being operated correctly. Given his current circumstances, Turner didn't have a lot of confidence in either being true. So even if the others were looking for him, the only way they'd be able to find him, or he them, was if they happened to end up in the same present moment—and checked their locator screen to realize it. So he had no alternative but to take the slow path into the future, and the slow trek through this desert.

He lifted his eyes to the small peaks ahead that were gradually drawing closer as he kept on trudging along. If he actually made it that far, he'd have to worry about getting over or through those mountains—but before then he should probably be looking for water. If he couldn't find some, he wouldn't be long for this world.

Likely there were ways to find water in the desert, if only he knew what those were. Some of these plants might yield enough water to sustain him, but he didn't know which—and many of them might be poisonous, not that he worried about that any more than he did about the snakes and scorpions slithering and scuttling about. But he knew some of these plants had hallucinogenic properties, and he wasn't sure what effect they would have on his system. He wasn't desperate enough to risk it, yet. Losing control of himself in these circumstances could quickly turn fatal.

He continued walking for hours, trying to keep his mind focused on watching his step, and avoiding looking at his watch. The night grew colder, but exertion warmed him up. His thighs and calves began to burn, and a thin sheen of sweat trickled across his brow. No doubt speeding his dehydration. And he had still seen no inkling of the presence of people in any direction as far as his eye could see. *How much of this will I have to endure?*

Chapter 2

The exertion that warmed him now would likely kill him if he kept going through the day. He finally paused for a brief rest and checked his watch. Daybreak was getting near. He would need to stop not long after that, but before he stopped he needed to locate shelter of some sort. Otherwise, the sun and heat would make quick work of him. He compared the coordinates of his present position to the place he had landed. He had been heading in a southeasterly fashion. *I trust that's the way You wanted me to go.*

With a deep breath he forced his legs to move—one step after another to make progress toward the smaller peaks. He'd been gradually angling toward those and away from a larger range he was now sure lay to the east. Maybe he'd find water there as well as shelter. He hoped to find both. And prayed he'd be able to make it that far.

As he kept going at a steady, even pace, Turner smiled at the irony. Before joining this research expedition, back when he'd been a young preacher, he had often talked about 'wilderness experiences' that tested and refined a believer's faith. But he'd never had one himself, not until now.

Whether it had been evangelism or academics, everything had always come easy to him. Maybe he would appreciate that more, after this. He believed what he was going through would make him strong

—if he got through it at all. For that, he knew he'd need a miracle. *You'll have to provide at least one of those if you want me to survive this.*

By the time the harsh yellow light began to glare over the higher peaks in the east, Turner was climbing into the rocky foothills to the south, making his steps a little surer, even if it required more physical effort to ascend. He could also see clearly now as he scanned his surroundings looking for shade, but the same sun that helped him see began baking him. He needed to find shelter before the sun rose any higher in the sky.

With the sun also came more life. Turner spotted some kind of antelope on a far hill, but mostly it was insects, crawling and flying and buzzing all over the place. As the sun continued to climb, those bugs became more annoying, and the air around him became a pulsating oven. If he had found somewhere that looked comfortable enough, he might have lain down and let the desert do its work.

He had noticed a few overhanging outcroppings —but none with enough room to rest under—and a few tight clefts he might've been able to stick half an arm into. It was nearing noon, and he was starting to feel disoriented. Loopy. Half-baked, even.

He thought he was laughing when he rounded a bend and saw a hole in the rock almost big enough to call a cave. He scrambled up to reach it and saw

Chapter 2

he would just be able to cram himself into the sweet shade, and there was no indication the place was the habitual abode of any particular creature, so at least he wasn't intruding on another's sanctuary.

He had to fold himself almost in half to squeeze inside, and he doubted he could get any real rest in that position. But he'd found shelter. Turner knew he might not last the day even so, but he comforted himself with the thought it would take long enough for his body to be found there that his identification might be taken seriously, that Verity would find out she'd been widowed.

He had hope, though, that when night fell again he'd be able to move on—keep going until he found what he needed. And he'd never been disappointed in his hopes. Yet. *But Lord, I don't think I can take another night like that.*

With those last thoughts in his mind, he laid his cheek against his knee and promptly fell asleep.

Chapter 3
A Walk in the Park

September 9th, 1912 San Francisco

PAGE squinted in the sudden bright light and wobbled a little as her heels sank into some thick grass. She blinked rapidly as her eyes tried to adjust to the sun shining in them. Her mind was slower to adapt. It had been ten in the evening a moment ago, and it should still be that, or thereabouts.

Whirling around, a bit unsteady on her feet, she took in the well-kept grass, the multi-colored banks of flowers, and the variety of trees. They'd landed in a park. She turned around again, but she didn't see any of the others. *Where's Matt?*

She'd had enough experience of being separated from him when they Traveled—but it shouldn't have

Chapter 3

happened, not when they'd been in physical contact when they left two thousand two. Maybe the difference was because they'd Traveled a whole ten years in one hop. But if there had been one thing they had been able to rely on, it had been arriving at the same part of the day-night cycle they'd left from. Not this time though. *Matt said he was sure that he had fixed the professor's device properly.*

Something clicked in her brain, and she looked down at her own watch—which told her it was ten in the morning on the ninth of September. In nineteen hundred twelve. Which would be a Monday. They'd landed almost one hundred years off course.

Checking her latitude and longitude, she swiftly calculated her position—the city of San Francisco in the state of California—and it looked like she'd landed in Golden Gate Park.

Orienting herself in time and space helped. She started thinking more clearly. Matt might have materialized on the opposite coast, in Chickadee where they were supposed to have arrived. She flipped to the locator screen and her mental gears froze. Page saw no blip and no red bar. Meaning no Matt in this time anywhere, or any of the others. Something had gone terribly wrong. She needed her brain to begin processing better.

There were any number of problems she should be dealing with right away. She started by focusing on one thing at a time. Her watch. Digital watches would be an anachronism here in the early twentieth century. She slipped the band off her wrist and held it for a moment—there was no one near to see, and some sort of shrubbery shielded her from view. *Where is Matt?*

She'd already oriented herself and had no need of the watch to keep track of her own location—and since none of her fellow Travelers were in this same time, the locator app was useless. The cash she carried had been printed decades in the future, and all those bills would also be useless to her. She needed money she could spend. She'd have to make getting to the bank her top priority, whatever that took—the nearest branch might be hundreds of miles away— her watch would know.

Page flipped to the resources screen and found there was a branch of her bank in the San Francisco of this era. She memorized the address, then generated the trust access code for today's date and memorized the twelve-digit alphanumeric before stuffing the watch into her jeans pocket—she'd gotten all she needed from it. Then she stepped out into the clearing to observe the people in the park. *Jeans.*

Seeing a group of young men wearing light suits broadly striped in tan and red with straw boaters on their heads, and a couple of women with the multilayered full-length skirts and short tunics of the pe-

Chapter 3

riod—and those monstrous hats—Page realized that her own apparel would not be considered appropriate. There was nothing she could do about that until she had money to go shopping though.

Wherever Matt was, he'd be trying to locate her, and the professor's device would pinpoint her spatiotemporal coordinates. They'd tested that, but that didn't mean he could Travel to her. That watch had clearly failed to work properly, so she couldn't rely on his being able to get to her. She'd have to begin heading back to the twenty-first century on her own. *But first the bank.*

She needed directions, but those conventionally attired ladies would likely snub their noses at her—the young men, on the other hand, looked outgoing and friendly. They would surely help her. One was already running toward her. He came and grabbed her arm—he must've thought she was having a dizzy spell or something, when it was just that these high heels weren't suited to walking in the park.

"Say, miss. You look as if you'd like some company."

Page smiled. He seemed eager to help her out—he might even give her a ride to the bank. Unfortunately, those two formidable-looking women who'd been walking nearby were swiftly bearing down on them. One of those ladies folded up her parasol and whacked the arm of the young man who'd grabbed

Page, forcing him to let go. She used it again to hit him over the head, knocking his hat to the ground.

"Shame on you, you young scoundrel. Can't you see she's a lady?"

The man glared at his parasol-wielding attacker while reaching down for his hat. "The 'lady' wasn't objecting."

The woman who had hit him raised her weapon as if she was about to hit him again, and the young man ran across the grass back to the friends he had left. The other woman glared at his retreating form and muttered, "Disgraceful."

The first woman unfurled her parasol again and held it out to share its shade with Page, and the other lady looked her up and down with an appraising eye before making introductions. "My name is Margaret, and my violent friend is Nancy."

"I'm Page. I don't suppose you'd be able to help me with some directions?" It would be a long slog to make her way a hundred years into the future, three years at a time. She'd need plenty of funds.

"Just as I thought. You must've come from one of those artist colonies up the coast. But surely you know that, whatever you might get away with wearing on those communes, such apparel will only get you into trouble here."

"Yes, of course. But I need to go to the bank before I can shop for another outfit. If you could—"

Chapter 3

"Wearing pants is daring enough, but blue jeans—I suppose that's some kind of statement. Support for the working classes or something? Which I applaud, of course, but anyone with any discernment can see you've got money. The quality material and the superior cut of those jeans could come straight from Paris—though I have a difficult time believing even the French would design something so form-fitting as to be positively indecent."

When Page could finally get a word in, she tried again. "I don't *have* money. But I will, after I get to the bank. Then I'll buy more appropriate clothes." And fashionable garments as well. Thankfully, any money she got from the trust stipend would remain valid tender as she Traveled forward in time. She'd have to remember to set up a proper account before rushing on.

Nancy smiled in sympathy, but Margaret shook her head. "You simply can't go walking into a bank looking like that. You must be feeling dizzy to even think such a thing—that would be the sun."

Margaret shifted her own parasol to share some of *her* shade with Page, who was beginning to resent being treated like a delicate flower. "I appreciate the advice but, like I said, I have to visit the bank—to get money—before I can go shopping."

"Nonsense. Nancy and I will take you to a little boutique we frequent and buy you an outfit to wear to your bank." She must've seen the look of distaste on Page's face. "Not a loan to be paid back, simply a gift. What's the point of having money if you don't use it to do some good?"

Page sighed. "I need to get to the American International State Bank on Montgomery Street."

"Certainly. That's in the financial district. They are relative newcomers—not being one of the banks that moved in decades ago to take advantage of the gold rush. They came in following the great earthquake, to help with the rebuilding."

Page looked around the park. "Which way is the financial district?"

Margaret took her by one arm, and Nancy took the other, and they started marching her across the grass. "We'll take the cable car—they're such fun—up Market Street to Union Square to get you those clothes we promised. Once you're properly attired, we can continue on to Montgomery Street and your bank. Or maybe you'd like to come to our house for a bite to eat first?"

Page shook her head. "I just arrived, and I need to settle my finances first, and rent a room. Maybe, if it doesn't take too long at the bank, I could come visit you afterwards." She knew she'd require sustenance after dealing with the bank manager.

Margaret nodded. "By the time we've shopped, and you've finished with your bank, it'll probably be

Chapter 3

just time for afternoon tea. We'd be delighted. Our house is on Nob Hill—we'll point it out for you when we pass by."

Nancy scowled at her friend. "Your house, Margaret, not ours."

"Not that nonsense again, dear." She turned to Page. "You live off a trust fund, don't you? So does Nancy, though she gets around that."

"Thanks to you." Nancy looked at Page as they stalked across the park. "Margaret became my trustee after her father passed."

"One of your trustees, dear. There's always that dusty old lawyer, but we took care of him."

Page had to ask. "Took care of him?"

Margaret smiled. "I got him to increase her allowance under the trust. Told him she'd have a better chance of catching a husband if she could afford to run a proper household on her own. He agreed—then once it couldn't be changed without my agreement, Nancy moved in with me. Now she can spend her money however she wants."

"I see."

"Now, about 'renting a room'—I'm sure you can do better than that. I don't know how much you get and I don't want to pry, but as a woman on her own you need a house with a staff, preferably. There are a few higher-class hotels though. A nice suite, with the hotel providing service, might be alright."

It was all a little overwhelming, but at least her companions weren't badgering her with questions—Page could just let them keep making their assumptions and didn't have to think up clever evasions. *I can go to nineteen hundred fifteen as soon as I have money.* If Matt could not get to her, then—although she didn't have any inkling when or where he might be—she'd have to go to him.

She was still in a bit of a daze as they all reached the cable car station. The ride went by in a flurry of impressions as they dinged their way north and east through different sections of the city, until Margaret and Nancy were helping her down to a fashionable little shop. That perked her up a bit.

To get out of the sun and away from all the stimulation of the novel sights and sounds was refreshing. Perusing the selection of short tunics and hobble skirts was fun. But she drew the line at corsets, or even a girdle—she felt she was slim enough not to torture herself to achieve a tiny waistline.

What really scandalized the saleswoman, not to mention Page's two companions, was her issue with hats. "But you have to have a hat."

Page shook her head. "God gave me this glorious head of hair—why would I want to hide it with a hat? Especially one of these fashionable monstrosities." The saleswoman made as if to faint, and Page accepted a hat. *I don't have to actually wear it.*

Chapter 3

When the three women walked to Montgomery Street, Page was wearing her hat. The one they had chosen, over her strenuous objections, looked like a multi-layered chocolate cake with little red roses on the rim. When they all approached the modest five-story brick edifice that was the bank, Page sighed in relief.

She turned to her two new friends. "Thank you for all your help. And this wonderful outfit." Minus the hat. "But you've already gone to enough trouble on my account. I think you can safely leave me here in the hands of my bankers."

Margaret reached over and patted her hand. "If you say so, dear." She pressed a card with some ornate calligraphy into Page's palm. "I'm not sure you paid attention when we pointed out the house. This has our address, and if you do decide to come to tea, we'd be pleased."

Page smiled. "Thank you. And I expect I'll take you up on that offer." In addition to the food, hopefully the two women would be a good source of data for her dissertation.

After all, she had come back in time in the first place to study the courtship rituals of the twentieth century. She couldn't pass up this opportunity. Setting things up with the bank would probably take a few days—enough time to collect some good information before moving forward.

Page kept nodding at the two women until they were gone. Thinking about researching dating customs reminded her that Matt wasn't there—to help with her observations. She would just have to make do without him.

With that thought, she steeled herself and went into the bank—the hardwood floors gleamed, along with well-polished counters, but the Spartan atmosphere was a distinct departure from the grandeur of the main branch in New York City. Or at least as it would be eighty-five years from now.

Every eye in the place turned to stare at Page as she strode across the lobby, casting her own glances around until her gaze lit on a tall, thin bespectacled man who'd just stepped out from a back office. He looked like a banker. Indeed, he might almost have been a twin to Mr. Hemmings, her banker in the future. She nodded at him.

The man moved rapidly to meet her, looking at her left hand before addressing her. "How may I be of assistance, miss?"

"I'm a Travelers' Trust recipient, and I'm here for the yearly stipend."

"Travelers' Trust, miss? I can't say I'm familiar with that."

Page sighed. The professor had set up the trust in the mid-eighteen hundreds. Perhaps this branch was simply too new. "Your bank not only adminis-

Chapter 3

ters the trust, but you're trustees as well. If you call the main branch in New York, I'm sure they can give you all the information."

The banker blinked rapidly. "Call? On the telephone?"

Page sighed again. "Yes. You do have a phone? Surely they're not that new?"

"Of course we have a telephone—it's a most useful instrument—but to call all the way to New York? Someday, maybe soon, we'll be able to talk to people that distant, but to contact the main branch I'll have to use the telegraph."

"Well? What are you waiting for?"

Nodding to himself, he left her standing there—in the middle of the lobby—while he walked back to a large open-air room behind the teller windows.

Page sauntered over to the side where she could see what he was doing. At one table a clerk sat with a telegraph machine, already tapping away with the banker looking over his shoulder. Hopefully all this rigmarole would not take too long—she was looking forward to tea.

There was a single chair in front of a desk off to one side, where another customer sat talking to another bank employee. With no other obvious place to sit, Page stood there tapping her toe impatiently. Until she realized she was copying the sound of the telegraph.

A Walk in the Park

Several minutes later, the banker returned with his lips pursed. "Allow me to introduce myself. Mr. Pitt, at your service."

"Call me Page."

"Miss Page, I'm afraid this branch is not yet set up to confirm the eligibility of applicants for receiving the Travelers' Trust stipend. Now, you could go to the main branch in New York City, or—"

Page cut him off. "I can't take the time—"

And Mr. Pitt had the audacity to talk right back over her. "Or. Given the likely time-sensitive situation you may be in, the main branch suggests another process to confirm your eligibility. If you provide me the first four digits of today's access code, they'll give me further instructions."

"4YT8. But they really shouldn't be confirming with only a partial—"

Mr. Pitt held up a hand to forestall her. "That's not for official confirmation. They simply desire reassurance before proceeding."

Before she could ask what he meant by that, the man had scurried back to the telegraph room. She didn't check her watch, but it felt like forever before he returned with a clerk trailing behind him.

"Miss Page, they've asked me to send them a secured package with your specific request for stipend funds along with the full access code for today's date—and a copy of an impression of your thumb mark."

Chapter 3

The banker exuded an air of embarrassment. "I am afraid it's a requirement of the trust. For identification purposes, so we don't deliver your money to the wrong person—as if we would—and also for the future, should you wish to keep your funds in an account with the bank. We wouldn't usually go to this extreme ourselves, but as I said—"

Page began nodding before he finished his spiel and cut him off. "It's a requirement of the terms of the trust. I understand, Mr. Pitt. It's alright, but I'd like to sit down somewhere while we take care of all this."

"Of course. We'll go to my office. I'm afraid we will have to use an ink pad to transfer an impression of your thumb mark onto a card."

"I don't suppose I have much choice." She knew they didn't have pre-moistened towelettes back this far, but she supposed she could wash her thumb off somewhere, somehow before she went to Margaret and Nancy's house for tea. If she finished her business here soon enough.

"Once they've confirmed your eligibility, they'll send the funds you request to us, and you can set up an account if you'd like. In the meantime, they have authorized me to extend you a small loan while you wait."

Page sighed. She didn't want to go into debt. If she had to, she supposed she could impose on Margaret's hospitality for a few days. "I can get by for a couple of days until my money arrives."

Mr. Pitt goggled at her. "I'm afraid it will take a train at least five days to deliver your information to New York. Then there's the processing time needed by the main branch before they send your funds by train back here. It will take two weeks or more."

Page felt a little faint. "I suppose I'll have to be grateful for your loan, Mr. Pitt. I hope it will be sufficient."

"I'm afraid our cash reserves are rather limited. This poor city—having just gotten past an epidemic of bubonic plague, they then had to have this Great Earthquake. They've had so much rebuilding to do —of course, we've been happy to help with that, but it is a strain."

"Alright, I understand. I'm sure I'll make do— but let's go ahead and get my stipend request on its way. I don't want to wait any longer than I have to."

It looked like she'd have plenty of time to do her research after all. But by the time two whole weeks had passed, Page would surely be eager to move on, hopefully getting closer to Matt. *Where, and when, is he?*

Chapter 4
A Day Late

September 25th, 1912 San Francisco

MATT heard a horn honking and leaped backward by instinct before he knew where he was or what he was doing. A big, cobalt blue Model T sped through the space where he'd been standing, and he turned to watch it trundle off down the road. *I thought they were all black.*

Other cars chugged up and down the wide road they shared with some horse-drawn carriages, bicyclists, and a frightening number of pedestrians, who strolled up and down the edges of the thoroughfare. His attention attracted by a loud dinging noise, Matt looked in the other direction to see a cable car pulling its way up a cross street.

Making sure he was well out of the way of that terrible traffic, Matt ducked into the shadows of an alleyway and checked his watch—which confirmed the impression he'd gotten from what he'd just witnessed. They'd gone back in time, rather than forward, and by quite a bit. *Nineteen hundred twelve.* Somehow it was ten in the morning, and he'd managed to lose Page.

He switched over to the locator screen and was stunned to see no blip and no red bar, no indication of any other Traveler in any direction. So the question wasn't where he'd find Page, but when.

Flipping a few screens over to an app unique to this master Travel device, he saw her coordinates— exactly where she was in space and time. *Very useful.* While the locator app seemed to work in a way akin to radar, simply pinging off other devices then relaying limited information, this program could be 'tuned in' to a unique device, then pinpoint its precise spatiotemporal position. Without knowing the 'frequencies' of specific watches, it was still of limited utility, but he and Page had tested until he had locked onto her own device. And he had left it tuned to that frequency.

Page was sixteen days behind him and, from the similarity in latitude and longitude, in the same city. Wherever that was. At least it shouldn't be too difficult to find her—he only had to wait until she caught

Chapter 4

up with him. *That can't be right.* Maybe he needed to figure out where she'd be sixteen days after she'd landed here—which would be today.

That didn't quite make sense to him either, but he was having trouble thinking clearly. Although it had been ten in the evening just a few minutes ago, now it was ten in the morning—and at least from his brain's perspective, it required some coffee to start functioning for the day.

His hand reached into his pants pocket to check his change. But while his mind might not be operating at peak performance, it did manage to arrive at the realization that his funds from the future would not be considered legal tender. He needed contemporary cash even to buy himself a cup of coffee.

That meant going to the bank. Page hadn't considered it necessary or appropriate for him to have access to the Travelers' Trust, so she hadn't demonstrated exactly how it was done. He'd seen enough, though, to get the general idea—he'd experimented on his own and seen how simple the procedure was, so he was already familiar with what he had to do.

Matt considered that cable car, and the hilly nature of the geography around him, and concluded it was probably San Francisco he'd landed in. He toggled to the resources screen and a list of contemporary branch locations, then noted an address for the American International State Bank on Montgomery

Street in San Francisco—the only branch west of the Mississippi. He hoped he was right about where he was. Because traveling very far without any money would be quite a challenge.

He called up the daily access code for the trust and memorized it together with the bank's location. Then he stepped out into the street again and gazed at the passing throngs. Since his digital wristwatch certainly didn't belong in nineteen twelve, he rolled down his shirtsleeves and buttoned his cuffs. He'd do well to look as conservative as possible anyway.

Thankfully his clothes shouldn't really be an issue—his dress-casual shirt and slacks weren't up to the standard of formal three-piece suits many men were wearing, but seemed respectable enough compared with how the workers were dressed, if only he had a hat. He was certainly cooler and more comfortably attired than any of them. Maybe they'd assume he was a college student.

At least no one recoiled from him as he tried to ask people for directions. Fortunately he'd arrived fairly close to his destination, and after a few blocks he found himself on Montgomery Street approaching the modest five-story brick building that housed the bank. And it was late enough in the day for it to actually be open. Hoping they weren't already on a lunch break, Matt walked through the door ready to do battle with a banker.

Chapter 4

His first thought looking at the lobby confirmed the impression he'd formed from the outside—a lot less posh than the New York City branch he had visited in the future. But then the San Francisco of this era seemed like it was still holding on to the ghost of the Old West in many ways. The thin man in striped shirt and glasses, who'd been summoned by a clerk in response to Matt requesting to see the manager, certainly looked like a banker even if he was dressed differently. Interesting that in an age of more formal attire, this banker should dress so casually. Their banker in the twenty-first century always seemed as if he had just stepped out of this era of heavy three-piece suits.

Shaking his head, Matt focused on the man approaching him and attempted to imitate Page's past performance with bankers. "I am a Travelers' Trust recipient, and I have come to access funds from this year's stipend."

The man replied without batting an eye. "If you would give me your name, sir, and the first four digits of the access code for today's date?"

"Matt." He was confused for only a moment before he realized that Page's first action when she arrived sixteen days ago would've been to come here, for the same reason as he—which was why the banker was familiar with the request. Matt rattled off the first four digits and added, "Page has been here."

The banker blinked. "You know the lady? Well, I shouldn't be surprised I suppose, since you're both trust recipients. Of course, I'll need to confirm that with the main branch. You're in luck that I already know the correct procedure, after dealing with Miss Page, so this should go quite smoothly."

So Page had cleared the way for Matt. But that didn't answer the question of where she was now, or why she wasn't showing up on the locator screen as being anywhere. He was impatient to ask this man about her, but he didn't want the banker to clam up on him. He'd have to wait for the right time.

"Well, that *is* fortunate, as I'm rather in need of ready cash." And coffee even more so, but he could not have the one without the other.

The man made a moue of distaste, likely at such a bald statement of financial desperation. At least, that's what Matt imagined. He didn't have a lot of time to daydream though—the banker disappeared behind the teller windows and re-appeared several minutes later with a smile.

"My name is Mr. Pitt, sir. If you will follow me, we can take care of the details and send the request for your funds off to New York. I'm afraid I'll need to take an inked impression of your thumb first, and then it will require two weeks or more for the transfer." He gestured at a clerk, then led Matt to a back room with a wooden table and two chairs.

Chapter 4

Matt sat down and stretched his long legs off to one side. "I suppose there's no way to get my money more swiftly than that?" Seeing the banker sadly shaking his head, Matt copied the movement. "Alright. I'm sure Page will give me what I need to tide me over until the cash comes through. Do you happen to know where I can find her?"

Mr. Pitt stood and watched as the clerk entered and sat down across from Matt and took his thumbprint. "I'm sorry, but I don't. When Miss Page came in yesterday morning to finalize her account details, I got the impression that she was leaving town." He saw the look of disappointment on Matt's face. "But don't worry. I can offer you a similar small loan as I did her, while you're waiting for the funds from New York."

Smiling and nodding at the banker, Matt sighed on the inside. Now he knew why Page hadn't shown up on the locator screen—she'd Traveled away only the day before he'd arrived. And that display of her temporal location had been relative to his own. Not so useful after all. He needed to know where to find her, not where and when she'd already been.

"I'll appreciate the money. I don't suppose Page said anything about where she was headed?"

"I'm afraid not, sir. Although she indicated she would return to this bank, she said it likely wouldn't be for two or three years."

Matt nodded and kept his face blank. Of course Page would've Traveled into the future—she'd have had no idea when in time Matt was, so that would've been the reasonable course to take. And he knew by now how logical she was. He couldn't know for sure exactly when she'd Traveled to until fifteen days had passed, but then he would have to wait that long for his funds to come anyway.

Meanwhile the bank clerk, having finished with Matt's thumb, had slid a simple sheet of paper over, to be filled out for requesting those funds and needing the full access code for today—and along with it another form, a promissory note for the loan.

Mr. Pitt talked as Matt wrote. "We'll send your request along with a copy of your thumbprint to the main branch in New York by secure carrier for final confirmation. Then, assuming all is in order, they'll dispatch your funds back to us here, and we'll set up your account."

"At which point you'll get *your* money back and stop worrying I might skip town without repaying."

The banker pursed his lips for a moment in disapproval. Narrowing his eyes, he asked a question. "Do we have an address in town where we can reach you?"

Matt grinned. Bankers didn't have any sense of humor, especially when it came to money. "Not yet, but I'll let you know as soon as I know myself where

Chapter 4

I'll be staying. Since I'll want to be notified when *my* money has arrived." Neither Mr. Pitt nor the money meant much to Matt right now though—only getting to Page.

The clerk stood and handed the stipend request and Matt's thumbprint to the manager, who turned and gestured with them. "I'll see that these are sent off today. If you'll follow Mr. Jones to one of the teller windows, he'll withdraw the cash we're loaning you, in the denominations you'd prefer."

Stopping at the door and glancing back, Mr. Pitt smiled. "Miss Page requested half of the remaining stipend for the year—I hope that what's left will be adequate for your needs."

Matt kept grinning. "I'm not surprised she did that. I requested the rest—I'm sure it will be enough to pay back your loan and still meet the few needs I have." In this second decade of the twentieth century, that thousand dollars the bank was loaning him should go a long way itself.

He stood and followed the clerk out and across the lobby to stand in front of a teller window while Mr. Jones stood behind it, all without another word to Mr. Pitt. Matt made sure he got some of the cash in coins, for coffee.

Out the door and glad to be free of the bank, he strolled a few blocks over into an apparent market district. There he found a little café where he could sit at an outside table and watch people go by. And hopefully get a cup of joe and some serious thinking done.

He was tempted to repine. If only he'd landed a day earlier, or if Page had waited around one more day before Traveling, then he wouldn't have had to deal with the bank or figure out how to find her. It was no good wondering what might've been though —better to focus on what he would do now.

A hefty man with a big moustache and wearing an apron came out and hovered beside Matt's table. "And what can I get for you today, sir?"

"Just a cup of coffee, please."

The man's face fell. Apparently anywhere, anytime, only ordering coffee was disappointing. However, the stout fellow, who Matt presumed to be the proprietor, rallied with a smile. "It will be two bits, sir, for a cup of our fine coffee."

Matt goggled. "Twenty-five cents for one cup of coffee." Surely he'd heard wrong, and that included refills at least. "This is nineteen twelve."

The man's face was red, but he shook his head. "What does the year have to do with it? Our brew is quality. If that doesn't matter to you, you can find a cup of swill somewhere for only ten cents."

"Ten cents!?"

"It's the Coffee Trust. These bankers monopolize the exchange and charge exorbitant prices, leav-

Chapter 4

ing us to pass the cost on to our customers. So why doesn't the government bust up this monopoly like they've done the rest?"

Matt smiled and shook his head. "I don't know, but as I need a good cup of coffee..." He took some change from his pocket and set a quarter on the table. He'd wait to order a second cup until he'd seen if their brew really was quality.

The man took his two bits. "Milk or sugar, sir?"

"Black, please."

"Right away, sir." He returned several minutes later with cup and saucer.

Matt took a small sip of the hot liquid and nodded his approval. If he was going to have to pay so much for coffee, it ought to be worth it. And it *was* halfway decent coffee. He took a few more sips and waited for his brain to warm up.

When he felt he could focus, Matt first considered Page—she had arrived far from their intended destination with no way to know when or where he might be. And she wasn't the type to sit around and wait for him to find her. So she'd done the only reasonable thing in her position—she'd started back to the future. After waiting two weeks to make sure of her funds going forward.

Probably she'd Traveled the full three years her leader device allowed, since she had a very long way to go. But Matt would know for sure in fifteen days, when he'd been here as long as she had. Though he wasn't sure why the professor's device was showing their relative positions in time as if a fixed relationship existed between their personal timestreams. If there was some way to adjust the 'temporal tuner' to display where and when Page was in his relative future, Matt didn't know. And he couldn't chance fiddling with it, not when he'd learn exactly where and when she'd Traveled to in a couple weeks anyway—he still had a lot to learn about time-travel mechanics. When he did find out her new coordinates, he would want to jump ahead in time to meet her. But he couldn't do that either.

The way their ten-year jaunt into the future had gone so horribly wrong, Matt didn't dare Travel using the professor's watch, not until he could be sure he'd fixed it. *What if I went backward in time again, instead of forward?*

He didn't hold out much hope that he could repair the device. Before they'd left he had inspected every nanometer of its interior structure—there was no more physical damage to be fixed. It had to be a problem with the programming, and while Page did not seem to have any difficulty working in the base thirty-two code it used, Matt found it challenging in the extreme. Either way, he still didn't really understand how the technology actually worked. It would be too risky to use until he did.

Chapter 4

Thankfully Matt had another way to reach her—one that would require phenomenal patience on his part—the slow path. Once he knew when and where Page would appear, he only had to make sure he was there when she arrived. The location should be San Francisco, since that would be where Page would've left from. But he would not count on anything anymore. Besides, he'd had personal experience of that particular feature not working properly.

But even if Page popped up on the other side of the globe, Matt should be able to get there in the two or three years he'd have to wait. And he'd have the money from the trust as well as all that time. When she materialized wherever she was going to, he'd be there to meet her. But just in case he missed her, he ought to leave a message for her with Mr. Pitt when he returned to the bank.

That way if Matt *wasn't* there when she landed, she'd wait for him. Hopefully.

Chapter 5
Nye and the FBI

May 15th, 2003 Midtown Manhattan

NYE walked down the deserted hall with the same sense of wonderful nervous tension she had experienced every day for the last two weeks. With the hotel's fourth floor all to herself—and not a chaperone in sight—she was all on her own. The Travelers had taken the entire floor for themselves when the trust had purchased this place, even though they had no need for so much room—twelve luxury suites. They had wanted the privacy.

Now, since everyone else had left the present to gallivant around time, there was only Nye. And Anya and Tate, though they would spend most of their days at the house up in Chickadee, only visiting the

Chapter 5

city occasionally—to check up on Nye. Anya had already called to say she'd be occupying her rooms at the Hotel Ngaio this weekend. Nye didn't want her work interrupted, but Anya had agreed to begin the summer a month early, so she couldn't complain.

Nye passed by the elevator and took the stairs to the lobby, pressing her index finger to the bridge of her glasses on the way down to activate the recording function. As she headed for the exit, she pivoted her head to take in the employees and guests in the lobby. The employees were unaware that she sort of owned the building—Mr. Hollingsworth, representing the trust, had hired a manager to run everything for them. It might be interesting to analyze changes in the personnel at the hotel, or the shifting population of the guests and more permanent residents. If she could ever find the time.

Then she was out on the sidewalk, all alone in a city of over eight million. She shook her head as she thought of the work involved in keeping track of the population of New York City. She didn't envy whoever had that job. How could there ever be an accurate count of how many people lived here?

Everything was in constant flux. Nye had a difficult enough time trying to document the layout of the city. She had spent the past two weeks focusing on Times Square—and would probably need at least two more weeks to finish the job—and after that she would need to track any changes. She took a different route to and from Times Square every day in order to make a new recording of areas she had studied already. Then every evening she would analyze that video to note any changes.

Nye walked down each bustling block swiveling her head to make sure she recorded the full sweep of every street. Her glasses chronicled the people too, but her interest was in the buildings. They were the bones of the city. They gave it shape and structure.

But there was a gap in that skyline, and Nye had not anticipated the visceral reaction she would have to not seeing the Twin Towers. Though it had been the impact of this city's future ruins that had caused her to make the ancient metropolis her special subject, so she shouldn't have been surprised.

Her mind shied away from imagining what people had gone through during those attacks, painful enough to think about the damage to the buildings. So Nye distracted herself by paying attention to the perpetual construction she saw everywhere. Not rebuilding—just the everyday business of the city adjusting to its changing needs.

Thankfully, Anya hadn't insisted Nye come into the city to volunteer in the aftermath of 9/11. She'd actually ordered Nye to stay away, saying she'd only be in the way—which would have been insulting if it hadn't been true.

Chapter 5

Her long, circuitous route finally brought Nye to Times Square. She stopped as she always did, turning in a full circle to appreciate the magnitude of the glaring, gaudy display. The multitude of brightly lit, giant, multi-colored neon signs flashing everywhere was less impressive, though, since she had learned it wasn't an organic phenomenon but rather one mandated by regulation. With all the mismatched, artistic architecture, and the throngs of tourists, even at this early hour, it was terribly stimulating. Nye kept out of the way of the foot traffic as much as possible. It had certainly been much more peaceful studying the city's ruins.

She examined the buildings one by one. Before she'd begun her detailed study, she'd assimilated all the information she could find from the library and online about the layout of New York and the history of the more impressive landmarks. There was nothing like looking at them in person though.

Whether they were the renovated remnants of a former version of the city or more modern marvels, Nye found them all worth her interest. But the current occupiers didn't seem to pay much attention to the structures they inhabited. She'd tried questioning some of them, but none seemed to know even as much about their buildings as she did.

She'd found several with an awareness of their building's architectural history, but nobody with an appreciation for material stress tests or load balances. Everyone appeared to think their buildings were earthquake proof though.

Nye did not doubt that the newer structures had all been built in strict accordance to the latest standards in engineering—or that the older buildings had all been retro-fitted. *What good did it do them?*

Shaking her head, Nye walked up to one building and pressed her hand against the surface of the outer wall, so glossy it looked like plastic. But it was only a carbon composite material and not even part of the actual wall—just decoration. She moved on to where she could touch the brick that really gave the place its solidity. Feeling that sense of permanence, it was easy to see how people had fooled themselves into thinking it would all last forever.

She felt a firm hand on her arm. Then someone was flashing credentials in her face as they grabbed her other arm and lifted her to her feet. Young men in suits, and one, an Agent Burke of the FBI according to his identification, spoke.

"You need to answer some questions, miss."

That was all she heard before they marched her around the corner and into a waiting black SUV that already contained two other men and one woman—presumably a female agent—who was in the front as their driver. The two who had taken Nye sat her on the back seat between them.

Chapter 5

One of the FBI agents had already removed her belt pouch without her noticing, and was handing it over to another agent as the tires screeched and the SUV sprang into motion. Nye watched as this older man, with gray in his hair, examined her bag and its contents.

"One key chain, with four keys. One long wallet with a state ID card and cash. Four hundred thirty-two dollars. And some loose change in the bottom." He handed her bag over to the fourth agent who had been making notes. "You can count the change."

Nye was glad that she'd gotten into the habit of leaving her watch in the hotel room safe. "This is a lot different from the last time I was arrested."

Their expressions were all blank, so she blinked rapidly to activate one of the analytical programs in her glasses to decrypt their microexpressions. Dismay. Consternation and surprise. And amusement from the older agent. There was no direct response to her comment though.

The one agent finished counting her coins, then noted down the exact amount and quickly reviewed the meager inventory. "No notes, and there doesn't seem to be any recording equipment."

The older agent shook his head. "We'll see."

Nye was still wondering what this was all about. "Can you at least tell me what it was I did wrong this time?"

The older agent looked at her with hard eyes. "I think we'll wait until we get to the FBI field office to have our discussion, Miss Nye Walker. I'm Special Agent Coulter, by the way."

She sighed. She couldn't see why they wouldn't tell her now why they'd taken her into custody when they would have to inform her eventually. Wouldn't they?

Turning her head to look out the tinted window, she saw they were headed south into the Downtown Civic Center. They drove to Foley Square and past a large group of people doing Tai Chi exercises, right up to the monstrous glass and concrete lattice of the Javits Federal Building.

Nye was hustled out of the SUV and in through a side entrance. Inside, she was directed to some sort of scanning machine—not a metal detector, but rather an advanced full-body scanner. Special Agent Coulter took the glasses off her face, and the female agent patted her down, and then they propelled her into the space where the machine would attempt to analyze her.

A technician operated the equipment. The machine hummed, the lights flickered, and Agent Coulter frowned. "Is everything alright?"

"Yes, sir. Must be an issue with the power company. Anyway, I'm getting a full readout, so everything is working properly."

Chapter 5

Special Agent Coulter was busy closely examining Nye's glasses. "And?"

"There are no transmitters or listening devices. And no traces of explosive material of any kind, and no radioactivity."

The man looked like he had more to say, but the agents were already marching her down the hallway to an elevator. They still held her by the arms. Rather firmly.

"Is this really necessary?" she asked. "I'm willing to cooperate. With whatever this is about."

They didn't let go of her or respond to her question, but at least when they got to the elevator doors they put her glasses back on her face. That technology was impenetrable, thankfully, unlike the watch. And Nye had a feeling she'd need her glasses—since she would have to get out of whatever trouble she'd gotten into on her own. This was an opportunity to prove she no longer needed a chaperone.

The elevator whisked them all up and deposited them in a clean-smelling carpeted lobby, where the agents then whisked her down a long corridor into a spacious interrogation room. At least she supposed it had to be that. There was a rectangular table with chairs on opposite sides, and a large mirror set into one wall.

The female agent and one of the men deposited Nye into a chair, then took up positions looming behind her. The agent still holding her belt pouch sat in one of the chairs across from her.

Special Agent Coulter took the chair beside him and nodded at Nye. "You've got clear glass in those frames—is it some kind of disguise?"

She shook her head. "No, I wear them to make myself look good." Which was the truth, just not in the way he was likely to think. She could watch her words just as well as Anya to avoid telling lies. She considered it a mark of her professionalism. "Now, what is this all about?"

"I'll ask the questions. Over the past two weeks you've been seen hanging around Times Square, all day, every day. You've been asking questions about various buildings—what materials were used in the construction, and about the entrances and exits and the layout of stairs and elevators. Are you assessing targets for an attack?"

"No, I'm interested in architecture."

"Then why have you been varying your routes to and from Times Square?"

"Because I want to learn about this city. There's a lot to take in." Had they been following her? That seemed the only way they'd know how she was coming and going. She blinked furiously again to start a subroutine search for reappearing faces in the video she'd recorded.

"Is this what you call cooperation?"

Chapter 5

Nye cocked her head. "I'm answering the questions you're asking. What more do you want?"

"How about we start at the beginning?" Special Agent Coulter paused as the door opened and a secretary walked in to hand him a very thin file folder. "Your legal name is Nye Walker, and you were born in Boartown, Indiana in nineteen eighty-three?"

"If you already know, why are you asking me?" Since he was asking about the history constructed to establish her legal identity, she blinked furiously to bring those 'facts' up on her glasses.

"Yes, we already know a lot about you." Opening the file in front of him, he scanned the contents. "Though I find the things we don't know about you much more interesting. While your birth certificate is on file with the state of Indiana, and we found an announcement of your birth in the Lafayette paper, there are no hospital records for you in the area, at all. Not even for your birth."

Nye frowned. Either they had worked very fast or already had a file on her. "I wasn't born in a hospital. Most women where I come from don't bother with going, unless there's a problem with the pregnancy. And I've never been sick."

He glanced at his file again. "This Boartown has a population of twenty-eight thousand, but we can't find any other records of your existence there. How do you explain that?"

Nye shook her head. "Is it my fault if you have trouble finding my records? I'm not very impressed with the information you *have* compiled. Almost all of those twenty-eight thousand are hogs—a fact you didn't seem to be aware of."

"Hogs?" Agent Coulter struggled trying to contain himself. "Are you telling me they count the pigs as part of the official population of the city?"

"Yes. They aren't allowed to vote of course, but a local ordinance does grant them the right to freely assemble."

At that point her glasses popped up with results showing two fresh faces that could have been young federal agents appearing around her in the last few days. In the hotel lobby as well as on the streets of the city. So they had been following her.

Once Agent Coulter could control his facial features again, he continued. "While you have a social security number—applied for at birth—there's little information about you in the system. We can't find out where you went to school."

"I'm not surprised." And they wouldn't find any other records of her, all of which existed only in the far future.

"To be honest, Miss Walker, it's all highly suspicious. It's what we might expect to see if your identity were merely a cover that had been established a long time ago for someone to step into. Such as an

Chapter 5

agent of a foreign power. Are you truly an American citizen? And is Nye Walker your real name?"

She shook her head. "I don't know how I could prove who I am to you if you won't believe the official documentation." They likely would not believe her if she told them the complete truth either. And she certainly couldn't prove it.

"If we have to, we can interview your supposed relatives."

Nye squinted. Most of her 'relatives' would not have any idea who she was. She only had Matt and Anya to back up her identity, and Matt had taken off for two thousand twelve. At least Anya wouldn't be going anywhere. Nye realized that her default decision to take Matt's Walker surname along with Anya was a blessing. Unlike her fellow Travelers, it would give her a 'real' relative to back up her identity. "Go ahead. My cousin Anya lives outside of Little Piece in Chickadee County."

Special Agent Coulter looked through the file in front of him again and switched topics. "In fact, you are a complete blank as far as we're concerned. Until two thousand that is. You were picked up by the police at the New York Coliseum demolition site for harassing the workers there."

"I was only asking them questions."

"Your interest in architecture seems to be centered on buildings' weaknesses—how to bring them down? I'm not surprised the New York police took you in for a psychiatric evaluation. But I find it odd that you didn't have any identification on you at the time."

Not so strange, considering she'd had no identification at all back then. She smiled at the memory of her brief stint in the looney bin. "Do you happen to have that file? I never got the chance to see what the doctors said about me, and I have to admit I'm curious."

The agents across the table stared at her—while Nye recalled the reason she had been released from the facility so quickly. *Mr. Hollingsworth.* Nye had been the reason for the Travelers' Trust retaining an attorney in the first place. And while he might have been expensive, he was also effective.

And still on retainer. She sat up straight, blinking to bring up the contact information for the lawyer. "Look, have we cleared this up now? I'd like to get back to my study of Times Square." Something always seemed to be interrupting her research.

Special Agent Coulter stared at her. "I'm afraid we're not ready to let you go yet, Miss Walker. And we certainly don't want you heading back to Times Square."

"You haven't even read me my rights, or let me make a phone call or anything. How long do I have to stay here and submit to this interrogation?"

Chapter 5

"Suspected terrorists don't have a lot of rights—and besides, who would you call?"

"My lawyer. Crispin Hollingsworth. He has his practice in Midtown. Hollingsworth and Everett. I can give you the number for his direct line, and you can call him for me. And tell him I won't say another word to you until he gets here." Nye was only to contact the man in an emergency, but this was starting to look like one.

Special Agent Coulter stared at her first, then at the agent sitting next to him. Whatever passed between those two wasn't in words. Both men rose to their feet.

Agent Coulter gave her a look her glasses failed to interpret. "Thank you for your cooperation. We will be in touch, Miss Walker, if we have any further questions." Then he nodded at the other agent, who grabbed her bag off the table and handed it back to her. "And now Agent Burke will escort you from the building."

All the way down to the lobby and out onto the sidewalk, Nye was pondering what had happened to her. Although she understood the gist of the situation, too much had passed her by, and she didn't appreciate that at all.

Since her research routine had already been seriously disturbed for the day, she decided to return to the Ngaio and review the notes she'd taken. She should also apprise Mr. Hollingsworth of what she'd just experienced. Nye didn't need to tell Anya anything though—even if it did prove that Nye needed no supervision, Anya would only worry more.

Turning north and walking away, Nye observed her surroundings to continue collecting more information. Even if most of it was irrelevant to her real work, more data was always a good thing—and now she needed to find the time to analyze more of what she gathered if she was going to begin understanding these people.

Nye had a difficult time relating to her contemporaries from the future. She found the twenty-first century inhabitants of this ancient metropolis more perplexing still. But if she ran enough analyses, and the right ones, on sufficient information, she should be able to comprehend them. She'd have the rest of the summer to think of a way to convince Anya to let her stay in the city year-round—she would need the extra time.

Chapter 6
Though I Know I Shouldn't

June 30th, 2000 Midtown Manhattan

ANYA's first mistake had been not calling Ralph to come and pick her up. Not wanting to disturb Tate, she'd risen early and left a note on the kitchen table saying she'd gone into the city on unspecified business—which was true enough. Given that the hired car arriving would surely wake him, and she hadn't wanted to answer any of his questions about where she was going or what she would be doing, she'd bicycled into town and taken the commuter train in—with multiple delays it had pulled into Penn Station over an hour late. And time was of the essence.

Her second mistake had been choosing to walk instead of take a taxi, thinking that would be faster.

But while the streets had been clogged with traffic, it still would've been faster riding than having to push her way through the rush-hour crowds.

Anya ought to have remembered how difficult it was to move swiftly through Midtown at this time of day. Especially since these crowded conditions had been why she wouldn't come into the city more than necessary—which had been often enough. She had needed to spend considerable time and effort in the city to determine the precise location and the exact minute of the professor's accident. Eventually she'd been able to ascertain both.

At the time, the professor's death had upset her too much to notice details like street signs or building addresses. But that one horrible scene had been burned into her brain. She could see it playing over and over again in her mind, and by walking around the general area where they'd landed and matching what she could see to the background of those images, she'd been able to find the spot.

As for the time of the accident, she couldn't ask the police, who surely knew. And she couldn't learn it from Mr. Hollingsworth, not without arousing his curiosity—at least she hadn't been able to think of a credible reason to offer him. So she had ended up at the public library, combing through the old editions of different newspapers, until she'd finally found an article specifying the time of the accident—and that

Chapter 6

time was approaching fast. It had also given the location, meaning Anya had wasted a lot of effort.

She'd planned to wait until she was closer to the scene of the accident to Travel. But worried she was falling far behind schedule, in spite of leaving plenty of room for error, she'd darted into an alley and set her watch to the maximum three years into the past. Arriving on the morning of the professor's accident, she had found the sidewalks even more packed with pedestrians. The *traffic* was flowing faster, but that only made it more difficult to catch a cab. And now she was in a hurry.

Having Traveled back into her own past, if Anya didn't get to the scene of the professor's death prior to its occurrence, she'd end up spoiling her one and only chance to prevent it. She was not about to give up though. *I'm not too late yet.*

She wasn't very far from her destination, so she ground her teeth in frustration and pushed through the throngs, feeling as if she were swimming against the current as everyone seemed to be headed in the opposite direction. Anya had no other option but to soldier on block after block.

She told herself it had been a hopeless cause to begin with, because as much as she understood the practical application of the time-travel devices, she had always been somewhat fuzzy on the theory—but the professor had clearly said that what she was trying to do now was something that simply couldn't be done. Even so, John had been her mentor. She had to make the attempt.

Memorizing the map for this section of the city was one way she'd prepared, and it was helping her shave a few minutes off her time as she struggled to reach the scene. She came to an intersection just as the light changed and took advantage of it, crossing Columbia before turning north again. John had appeared in the northbound lanes right before he was struck and killed. So her plan required her to be on that side of the road.

When Anya had first dreamed of Traveling back to save the professor, she'd envisaged herself rushing out into traffic to push him out of the way, but it had not taken her long to realize that wouldn't work. It would all happen too fast.

If she waited to act until the professor had actually materialized, it would already be too late. Anya needed to act first. Knowing the minute of the accident, she could try running out into the road a little beforehand, but she doubted she could time it precisely enough to be sure, and she would only get the one shot. And she might just push him into the path of a different vehicle. Whatever she ended up doing might get her killed. If that was all she managed to do, it would be a horrible waste, but if she died saving the professor's life, it would be worth it.

Chapter 6

The others might miss her if she died instead of John, but he would've done such a better job of taking care of them than Anya had. So finding a way to rescue him, even at the risk of her own life, was what she had focused on.

Looking at what had actually happened, she realized that rather than removing the professor from danger, she needed to mitigate the threat he would face in the first place. So her rushing out into traffic just before he appeared was the right idea—but not in order to get to John in time. Her aim was to stop traffic.

When the professor had been struck and killed, so many vehicles had screeched to a stop that Anya remembered the street seeming almost like a parking lot. It had created the opportunity for her to go running out to John, where his body had lain across the back windshield of a taxi. She meant to reverse that dynamic. If she darted out into traffic right before he materialized, it should bring everything to a standstill and provide the professor with the chance he needed to orient himself and get out of danger. If only she could get close enough in time.

She glanced down at her watch. *Three minutes.* And she was still a block and a half away. Her skirt swirling around her legs, she began shoving her way more forcefully through the crowds, but to little effect. Time was running out.

Though I Know I Shouldn't

Having made her way down most of one block, Anya still needed to cross the next intersection. But when she glanced at her watch again, she saw she'd only two minutes remaining, more or less. It would have to do.

She darted out between two parked cars and into the paused traffic waiting for the light to change. Working her way around those vehicles she tried to run ahead into the intersection, but a barreling cab honked its horn and almost ran her down. It was a jolt. And she found she could no longer force herself to consciously run recklessly out into the path of the oncoming cars. So waving her hands in front of her, she waded out a bit at a time.

More horns blared and drivers raised their fists in anger, swearing at her, but most barely bothered to slow down. A taxi swerved around her, scraping the side of another. But Anya was looking ahead to where the professor would soon appear and almost made it across before the light changed and the cars in the northbound lane surged forward, toward and around her.

She ran forward, veering to the left and the right and trying to force the oncoming cars to slow down. Then a strange feeling swept over her, a kind of off-kilter déjà vu—and suddenly Professor John stood there, up ahead of her. Instinctively she called out. "Professor!"

Chapter 6

At the same time she heard the echo of her past self yelling the same thing from the other side of the street. *No wonder the professor had looked so confused.* And then history repeated as a big black SUV braked hard, slamming into John and sending him flying forward into a cab that was coming to a sudden stop further ahead.

Anya watched in horror as her past self ran out between slowing and stopping vehicles to reach the professor's body. The same scene she'd replayed in her head so many times. Only now she was watching it all from a different angle—one from which she herself was the cause of the accident.

The next minute her past self was running away from the scene of the accident, through the crowd of onlookers that had immediately formed. And Anya already knew what happened after that—or she had thought she did.

As she had stood there, a frozen obstacle in the middle of the street, the black SUV that had struck and killed John had lurched into motion. With tires squealing it jumped into the next lane over, cutting off a slow-moving cab. As it forced its way into moving traffic, Anya realized that the driver who had hit the professor was running from the scene.

While she had not been able to prevent the professor's death—perhaps had been inadvertently responsible for causing it—there was still a wrong she could right. Seeing it was available, she ran forward to the cab that SUV had just cut off, pulling a hundred dollar bill from her pocket as she went. Anya had tried to prepare for every eventuality. She had even taken the battery from Tate's watch in case she needed to Travel again in a hurry. Not that she expected she'd have to do that.

She pounded on the window, pressing the money against the glass and smiling. And as soon as the cabbie had unlocked the door, she slid into the back seat and handed him the cash. "You saw that black SUV hit and kill that man? And run? I need you to follow it."

The driver, an old man with gray crew-cut hair, took her hundred dollars and began racing forward even before he had turned back to see where he was going. "You ought to leave it to the cops, lady. But I want to earn the fare."

Anya winced as the taxi darted through a brief gap that had opened between a bus and a limousine. "Can you see him?"

"Sure I can, lady. In this traffic I would have to be blind to lose him."

Leaning forward, it wasn't long before Anya had caught sight of the hit-and-run driver for herself, at least saw a black SUV up ahead that the cabbie was clearly following. She hoped it was the right one. It didn't seem to be trying to lose them, but maybe its

Chapter 6

driver didn't realize he was being pursued—the traffic was not only thick, but thick with cabs that mostly looked alike.

She decided to risk questioning the cabbie. "Is that the same black SUV? Are you sure? I'm afraid I didn't notice any distinguishing characteristics."

He didn't bother to look back at her. "I've been keeping my eye on it ever since he cut me off, so yes I'm sure. As for any 'distinguishing characteristics', I think you'll find that on the front end—the blood of the guy he hit."

Anya grimaced upon hearing the professor's accident referred to in that way, but she said nothing. What she did was try to think where the hit-and-run driver might be going, and what she would do once she caught up to him. If she did.

Where that SUV actually headed for was a nondescript parking garage. "Follow him in, driver, and get as close as you can. Otherwise he might lose us in there."

The cabbie shook his head but turned in to follow. "He may not know we've been tailing him, but he'll figure it out if we get too close."

"I'm more concerned about what he might do in here if we lost track of him. There might be dozens of black SUVs parked in here, and if we had to check out each one, he could be long gone by the time we found the right one."

He might leave his vehicle to escape on foot, or he might circle up and around and down again and leave them examining every black SUV in the place—which was a dark and claustrophobic block of gray concrete. And as it happened, when they'd entered the parking structure, she'd already lost sight of the SUV ahead of them. "Can you see him anywhere?"

The cabbie shook his head. "I think I hear him up ahead, but that could be anybody. But I'm keeping my eyes peeled in case I get a glimpse."

Anya nodded, though the man wasn't watching her. "You do that, and I'll look for black SUVs that might've just parked." Except she wasn't sure how she could tell, other than getting out and feeling the hood to see if it was still hot. She'd do better to look and see if there was evidence of the accident on the front grill. "He has to stop somewhere."

"He may have come here just to dump the SUV. Likely it was stolen in the first place, and the police won't be able to trace it back to him."

"But if we find the right one, you *will* call to let the authorities know where they can find it? Even if the driver stole the vehicle, there must be evidence inside to identify him—fingerprints or DNA."

The cabbie shook his head. "I wouldn't expect the cops to go to that much trouble. Run the fingerprints to see if the guy's in the system, maybe, but I doubt they'll do any more than that."

Chapter 6

"If that's not enough to catch the culprit, I'll see to it myself." Surely the resources she had could be put to no better use than bringing this hit-and-run driver to justice. Not only for the professor. Others might be in danger if such a reckless and irresponsible person wasn't stopped. "But I hope we'll be able to follow him wherever he's headed, and then we'll call the police to arrest him."

They had wound their way up to the fourth level and were speeding between rows of parked vehicles when Anya spotted him. *It has to be.* A short, thin man was just walking away from a black SUV, walking with his head down and a suspiciously slow gait. Then he stopped in his tracks and looked up.

Anya cried to the cabbie. "That's him. Stop and let me out."

The taxi rolled to a halt, and the driver glanced back at her. "I don't think that's such a smart idea, lady. This guy might be dangerous."

"I could at least get a good picture of him." And before the cabbie could reply, she opened the door and hopped out.

Standing between the taxi's open door and this man, who'd stopped to stare at her, Anya raised her watch to capture an image before he could get away. Then she noticed his eyes—cold and hard, and still staring at her. She'd seen dead, empty eyes like that before, and she felt a shiver run up her spine.

The otherwise nondescript man smiled and lifted his arm to look at his own watch and then back at her. With a shock, Anya realized he was confirming her as the blip on a locator screen.

He's got one of our watches. Turning, she dove back into the back seat of the cab. "Go. Now. Get us out of here." The driver hit the gas and the taxi flew forward.

Almost numb with shock, Anya yanked the door closed as the taxi rounded a corner, making for the exit. Three floors below. She heard a squeal of tires and glanced back. She couldn't see the black SUV, but she knew that had to have been the sound of it pulling out to come after them. Then she thought to look down at her watch and check her own locator app—which indicated another Travel device still in range behind her.

She checked the picture she'd taken of him, the picture of a killer. Not someone she recognized. It didn't take her long to run through the possibilities —of course, one of the others might have lost their Travel devices in the future or the past, but she only knew of one of their watches that was definitely unaccounted for. Kirin's.

According to Sam's letter, which had been awfully short on details, she didn't know what had become of Kirin's helper device when she died. Anya hoped that was the only watch on the loose. With it

Chapter 6

being unable to Travel on its own, the only problem was its ability to track other, similar devices—a big problem right now, though, considering who might be using it to track Anya.

With eyes like those, he had to be some kind of violent criminal, and she had no doubt he'd learned enough to use the locator screen. She needed to get away from him. That meant putting some distance between them, enough so she could Travel without taking him back to the future with her. *But how am I going to do that?*

The cabbie pulled out of the parking garage and into the street. "Where to now?"

Anya looked down at her locator screen to confirm that her pursuer was still in range. Then she looked up and saw the thick traffic. "I don't know. Let me think."

The man was too close behind her to shake easily, unless they could get to open highway, and even then it would be difficult. Getting to a train station or airport wouldn't help. He would probably still be close enough to board the same train or plane as she did, and how would she stop him? Somehow she'd have to figure out how to put over a hundred meters between them in a very short period. Then she had a brain wave.

"Drop me off in front of the Whitaker building, please. And then forget all about this."

Though I Know I Shouldn't

The cabbie glanced back with a frown. "Lady, I don't like to say I told you so, but I said it was a bad idea, what you were doing."

"Indeed. I should've left it to the police."

It was only as the taxi wound its way toward the Whitaker building that Anya wondered why she was being pursued. Whoever that man might be, clearly he knew enough about the watch he was wearing to track Anya—she thought she could safely assume he wanted to lay his hands either on Anya herself or on her device. *Can he possibly have guessed my watch can Travel? Had he already been tracking me?*

He'd been right there to run into the professor, and Anya couldn't consider that a coincidence. If he *had* been tracking anyone, it couldn't have been the professor or any of the others, because they'd come through just a moment before the accident. He had to have been following her.

Rather than worry about that, she needed to be concerned with getting away from the man, and the Whitaker building was just a little further down this street full of skyscrapers.

Exactly what she needed. Most, if not all, of the tall buildings had express elevators—to take people past the lower levels to the upper floors. She hoped her familiarity with the Whitaker would help her go quickly to one of the right elevators and get on, and without her pursuer getting on with her.

Chapter 6

The cab screeched to a halt on the other side of two parked cars in front of the main entrance to the Whitaker, and Anya popped out and ran for the big glass doors. She darted through a closing door and sprinted across the lobby's marble floor to the bank of express elevators. Making sure every call button had been pushed, she waited on her tiptoes.

As soon as she heard the ding and saw the light come on above one set of doors, she went straight to stand in front of them and pushed her way in as the doors opened and people started filing out. Pushing the button for the top floor, Anya relaxed.

This elevator only stopped at the highest floors, so even as she watched a few other people getting on and hitting other buttons, she didn't worry. None of them was the man with the eyes.

The last woman in hit the button for the forty-ninth floor and the doors closed. The elevator rose with a lurch and accelerated so fast Anya could feel her stomach dropping as they zoomed upward. The first forty-eight floors would be bypassed before she knew it. And since twenty floors would put about a hundred meters distance between her and the man chasing her, then she should be safe to Travel by the time it reached the forty-ninth. Or the forty-fifth.

This express elevator wouldn't stop at any floor below that, but if someone pushed one of those call buttons, it might stop before the forty-ninth, so she excused her way through the other occupants of the car to stand right before the doors. She had to wait until she could get off the elevator before she could safely Travel, but she didn't want to wait a moment longer than she had to.

Not wanting to waste any time, Anya set the coordinates on her watch to Travel the full three years into the future. Then she remembered to switch her used battery for Tate's fresh one.

Once Anya could Travel without taking this other watchbearer along to the future, he'd only be able to track the earlier version of Anya—and she hadn't had any problems with him in the past—so that was alright. And none of the others had mentioned having to deal with this sinister man, so *everything* was alright. And it would remain that way, because you couldn't change your own past. Though apparently you could cause it.

Her efforts to save the professor had been a disaster from start to finish. Once she was back in two thousand three, Anya could consider her failure and what, if anything, she could or would do next.

The bell dinged and the car settled on the forty-ninth floor, and the second the doors opened, Anya was stepping off onto plush carpet and into a large lobby. And then she Traveled.

Chapter 7
No One There

September 9th, 2012 Chickadee County, NY

VERITY knocked on the door one last time before walking along the porch and peering in through the living room windows to confirm what was only too obvious. The place was deserted. More than three months after Verity should have appeared here with the others. She didn't know what had happened in the interim, but no one was here waiting to see if she showed up. Not even Turner.

Without knowing where or when any of the others were, or whether they could truly track her with their watches, Verity had to decide what to do next. And that wasn't going to be waiting about an empty house for someone to show up someday.

Huffing and puffing noises made Verity turn to see Karat trundling around the corner of the house. Despite Verity's protests, the pregnant woman had insisted on circling the grounds looking for signs of life—apparently exercise was good for the expecting mother, even when she seemed about to pop. Especially when she'd been crammed into that two-door compact all morning.

They *had* stopped for a couple of rest breaks on their way. Three hours of mostly country scenery—lots of cows and horses—that Verity hadn't paid any attention to, because she'd had to focus on remembering how to drive. With the road and other drivers having first claim on her, she'd only half listened to Karat chatting about her parents and growing up Jewish in a Boston suburb. All the talk of the travails of pregnancy she had intentionally tuned out.

That very pregnant woman looked at the stairs up to the porch and shook her head. "I couldn't see anyone anywhere. Sorry, but it looks like nobody's home. Don't you have any idea where else to look for them?"

Verity sighed. She thought the rest were probably at the following summer. Or maybe in New York at the Ngaio. "Looks like they've gone for the summer, and they won't be back until May or June. The only other place I can think to check is in New York City."

Chapter 7

Karat leaned against the railing and smiled. "If you recall, I'm headed there myself. Why don't you drive me the rest of the way?"

Verity's nerves would be tested driving into the city, but she'd have to face it. "Of course."

"And you said you'd lived there before. Maybe you can help me find my husband's old friend?"

"We'll call it another trade. And yes, I *am* quite familiar with the city." As it had been ten years ago. "It should be simple to search for this person." Simple being a relative term. "You've got an idea where to start looking, I hope."

"He's somebody my husband met in law school, and supposedly he's got a practice in the city—a Mr. Crispin Hollingsworth."

Verity stared into space, trying to keep her face from showing her surprise. Hollingsworth had witnessed her wedding. If she could not find Turner or any of the others, the lawyer might be her next best hope for help. She looked down on Karat's glowing face. "Lawyers like to be found by potential clients, so I doubt it'll be too difficult to find this one."

Karat nodded. "I'd still appreciate your help."

But having begun to think about Hollingsworth had caused Verity's thoughts to veer off in another direction. "When you said you needed the help of a friend of your husband's, I assumed you meant help with expenses for the baby."

Karat's late husband had been a lawyer, though—and now she was seeking assistance from another lawyer, and one of Hollingsworth's caliber. It could be just another incredible coincidence, like the lawyer being one Verity happened to know, but Verity's antennae had started to quiver. "There's something else, though, isn't there? Some kind of trouble."

The woman's face flushed, and tears began rolling down her cheeks. "I'm sorry. It's been a couple weeks since Miles died, and I told myself that I was *not* going to cry any more. I suppose it must be the pregnancy—you know how it plays havoc with your hormones."

Verity shook her head. "No, I don't know, but I *am* sorry if I upset you. I didn't mean to. Go ahead and cry all you want."

That brought a smile back to Karat's face. "You didn't know. But I need to hurry up and get over it, for the baby's sake."

"I'm not sure you should ever *get over* losing a spouse."

Karat wiped her tears away with her hand. "I'm sorry. I forgot you're missing your husband too, but at least he's still among the living."

"To be honest, I don't know if he *is* still alive."

"How long has he been gone?"

"Ten years. I haven't seen him since the day after our wedding." And not only might Verity never

Chapter 7

see him again, she could conceivably never find out *if* he died, much less when or where or how. "How did your husband die?"

Karat had managed to stop crying. "I guess we could compete for most tragic story. Miles fell from the roof of the building where he had his office. The police said it was suicide, but they're wrong—I know my husband, and he wouldn't have jumped. And it couldn't have been an accident since he didn't have any reason to be up on the roof."

"Then, that only leaves..."

"I just couldn't understand it. And then a week after his death, someone broke into his office. They searched through his files—that's when I realized he must've been murdered. After that, I got the feeling someone was watching me, but I never saw them. I think they might be following me."

Verity sighed. "I wish you had told me all of this earlier."

"I should have told you before we started off together. But whoever they might be, I didn't think they'd have any interest in you—I hope I've not gotten you into any trouble."

"That's not what I'm worried about." Assuming these mysterious watchers did become interested in Verity, she imagined they'd have a difficult job just finding out who she was. Assuming they existed in the first place.

Verity was inclined to be skeptical. After all, impending motherhood, together with losing her husband in such a traumatic way, might've unbalanced poor Karat. But she pursed her lips to avoid voicing that thought.

It must've shown in her expression, though, because Karat blushed. "I know I probably sound paranoid. Maybe I am, but then when I think about—" She broke off whatever she'd started to say and gave Verity a sheepish look. "I should probably wait and tell Mr. Hollingsworth the details. Then I'll let him decide what to do."

"I understand, and that seems like the best idea to me. So let's go into the city and find him for you. As for anyone following—well, I wasn't looking, but there wasn't enough traffic on the road down to disguise the fact, if someone was following you."

Although anyone willing to break into a lawyer's office wouldn't balk at much. And if they were truly watching or following Karat, the only reason Verity could see for that was if they hadn't found whatever they'd been looking for. In which case, they might have attached a tracking device to the car, in order to follow at a distance. They could've installed a bug even.

Verity wanted to finish this conversation here, away from Karat's car. "Did you tell anybody where you were going, who you were going to see?"

Chapter 7

Karat shook her head. "I didn't dare. I couldn't know who to trust, so I didn't even let anyone know I was leaving at all."

Verity nodded. That was one advantage to paranoia—it came in useful if someone really was after you. So she likely didn't need to warn the woman to not talk about Hollingsworth, or anything else unfit for listening ears. It would just make her more nervous to mention it. Not a good idea—whether or not this turned out to be a delusion.

Verity had one more thing she wanted to say before they left. "Just in case we are being followed, I want to think about how we might lose them. Once we get into the city, just go along with whatever I'm suggesting. As if it makes sense, alright?"

"Alright." Karat levered herself away from the railing and waddled over to the car, to stuff herself into the passenger seat and wait.

Hoping the woman would continue to be amenable to her ideas, Verity got behind the wheel and buckled her seatbelt before starting the car. Driving down the little lane and turning back onto SR22 and heading south, the silence in the car was a distinct change from earlier, and uncomfortable, but at least it would give Verity the mental space to think. Karat just stared out the window.

When Verity realized she was repeatedly checking her rearview mirror for a tail, she knew at least part of her mind had credited Karat's tale. Though if anyone were following, she didn't see them.

What a lawyer might be able to do for this woman, Verity couldn't know, not without hearing more of her story. But still she didn't want to pry. What she did want to do was hand Karat over to Hollingsworth without bringing any trouble to his door—no more than she had to, anyway.

So though she remained skeptical, Verity tried thinking how best to lose anyone who might be following them. Focusing her attention on avoiding a wreck, she was able to spare an occasional thought. Anyone who'd been watching Karat would certainly know the make and model of her car, as well as the license plate number and probably the VIN. Even if there was no tracking device, this vehicle needed to be abandoned for alternative transportation.

Verity only hoped trying to convince the woman to give up her car didn't set her off. She hadn't observed any hormone-induced mood swings to rage, but a flood of tears would be nearly as bad. At least she had a good replacement vehicle in mind.

Thankfully, her wedding was only a couple days ago from Verity's point-of-view, so she still remembered the details of Turner's wedding gift. He'd taken her to the dealership to present it to her—for all the good she had thought she'd get out of it, living in the city and never driving. It had been the thought

Chapter 7

that counted, then. Now she appreciated the gift itself, and also that Turner had arranged for the car to be kept ready for her to accept anytime in the future —and since they'd planned on skipping the next ten years, it had seemed only prudent. Now it was positively providential.

So she wouldn't complain that it would've made more sense for Turner to wait to buy her a car until they'd arrived in twenty twelve. Instead, she would be grateful that she remembered where to find that dealership. And that there was a mall nearby.

So, in White Plains Verity changed to the Bronx River Parkway, then took that into the city, then got off the race course and headed for the massive parking garage attached to that shopping center she had recalled. After finding an empty place to park, she turned to Karat and winked. "I think we could both use a nice, long break before we make our way into Manhattan, don't you?"

Karat just nodded in relief and opened the door and began the process of extricating herself. Verity didn't want to imagine what it must've been like for the woman driving all the way across Massachusetts on her own. But in no time at all, Karat was out and headed for the mall entrance and no doubt the nearest restroom.

Verity hurried to catch up to her and spoke low as she came along side. "After you finish your business, why don't you go to the food court and take a good half hour to get a proper meal." A giant plate of nachos at a convenience store along the way had been the woman's lunch. Verity had made do with a microwaved burrito.

Seeing Karat nod, she continued giving her instructions. "When you finish, go to the big department store at the south end of the mall and shop for another half hour." Verity checked her watch to see the current time. "Then about a quarter past four, I want you to try slipping out the door to the back lot when no one's looking. Alright?"

Karat nodded, then glanced at her watch before charging ahead through the milling crowd to get to the restroom. Hopefully the woman had been paying proper attention.

With a mental shrug, Verity focused on the first task she needed to accomplish. Since anyone who'd been spying on Karat would now know what Verity looked like, she had to have a disguise of some sort. There was no point trying to camouflage the eight-months-pregnant woman, but Verity needed to slip away from the mall unnoticed for her plan to work.

It took her ten minutes to find a wig shop—then she found another store and bought a couple accessories. Twenty minutes later she was visiting a different restroom to transform herself. She exited the mall as a busty, bee-hived blonde—a gauzy rainbow

Chapter 7

scarf and pink purse glittering with rhinestones finished the look. She likely looked as if she'd stepped straight out of central casting, but she should be unrecognizable to anybody watching for her. That was what mattered.

Fifteen minutes from the mall, the sales people at the luxury-car dealership saw her waltz into their showroom. If they were shocked, they were far too professional to show it. As soon as she was inside, though, she ripped off the wig and scarf and stuffed them into her purse. And scanned the place for any familiar face.

Seeing someone who'd been here ten years ago, she stalked up to a large, muscular man with a ruddy complexion.

He looked older, naturally, but his manner was still hearty. "How can I help you, miss?"

"Since it's been ten years, I'll forgive you for not recognizing me, Mr. Venn. As long as you have *not* forgotten to take very good care of the car my husband bought me. Considering what it cost Turner, I presume it will be in pristine condition."

His face grew even redder. "Of course I haven't forgotten, you or your car—which has been lovingly maintained for you. If you don't mind my saying so, you haven't changed a bit in ten years, Miss Dervan. Or should I say Mrs.—"

"It is now, and still, Mrs."

"I'm glad you've finally come to your senses and come for the car. But it's ten years old now. Surely you'd like to trade it in for a newer model.

Verity sighed. "You're a salesman, of course, so I understand. But the only thing I'm interested in is driving away in my wedding present. That's not going to be a problem, is it?"

"You have your keys with you?"

She smiled. "Of course—it was a beautiful gift." Even if it hadn't been of any use until now.

"Then all you have to do is sign the delivery confirmation papers. Once you're satisfied it's in good condition."

He led her out to a side lot and showed her the silver Mercedes, where it sat among any number of shiny automobiles glinting in the sun, but she didn't bother to inspect it. She didn't have the time. "It's got gas in the tank?"

Mr. Venn looked pained. "Of course. To keep it in fine running order, we had to drive it regularly. It has almost a full tank."

Verity allowed herself to laugh. "Ready for that day when I would come to my senses? It must have taken me a lot longer than you imagined."

He managed a polite chuckle. "I'm happy such a fine vehicle will finally be appreciated."

Signing the paper he'd handed her and unlocking the driver's side door, she slid into the cool inte-

Chapter 7

rior. A nice change from Karat's compact. "And it will be appreciated, Mr. Venn. It will indeed."

Then she was grateful for the practice she'd gotten all day—she backed out of the tight spot without scratching any of the other cars. Then she pulled off the lot and out into traffic without hitting anything, or anyone.

Only a few minutes later, Verity was in the back parking area of the mall donning her wig and scarf again and liberally applying pink lipstick to go with the purse. Then she checked her watch. Everything had gone smoothly on her part. If Karat was following instructions, she should be waddling out at any minute.

Verity kept a close eye on the rear exit and started the engine the second she saw Karat pushing the heavy glass door open. The woman stepped out onto the sidewalk and looked around with an air of bewilderment—which became surprise when she saw the Mercedes slide up next to her and the back door pop open. Verity called out to her, "Hop in."

Though hopping wasn't actually an option, Karat did scramble into the car rather quickly considering her condition. She must not have looked at the driver, only recognized Verity's voice, because they were already pulling away when she got herself settled and finally looked up front and saw.

"Oh my word!"

Verity made a face in the rearview mirror. "It's a disguise, Karat. I should be free of anyone following me, and this car is clean. If anyone was watching you, hopefully we've given them the slip." And if not yet, then before they reached the Ngaio.

Karat leaned back and looked around the comfortable interior. "And this car?"

"A wedding present from my husband I had no use for until now." Of course, it had only been a few days from Verity's perspective. If she hadn't taken this mad trip ten years into the future, she probably would've picked up her car a lot sooner.

Karat shook her head in wonder but said nothing. Thankfully that silence reigned as Verity navigated her way into Midtown, focused on fighting the afternoon traffic. When she reached the Ngaio, she ignored the honking behind her as she stopped next to two taxis parked in front of the hotel, positioning the back door to give Karat a clear path between the bumpers to the front door.

Turning to speak to the woman, Verity made an effort to smile. "You don't want to be any more visible than you have to be. Just go straight to the elevator and ride up to the fourth floor—and if you see anyone there, tell them you're with me." That ought to surprise them. Though she didn't expect Turner or any of the others to be in residence. "I'll be parking the car and coming right behind you."

Chapter 7

After staying long enough to see Karat enter the lobby safely, Verity moved on. Twenty-five minutes later the elevator was depositing her on that fourth floor, where Karat was waiting. Alone. And cross at being left for so long.

Verity had her keys in hand and marched right to room 408 and opened the door after a peremptory knock. She waved Karat in ahead of her. "This is our suite—Turner's and mine. Please take a load off and feel free to make yourself at home."

The woman looked around the sitting room and levered herself into one of the wide leather chairs. "I don't understand. If you have these rooms, haven't you looked for your husband here before?"

Roaming through the remaining rooms to confirm her husband was not there, Verity answered as best she could. "It's a long, complicated story. Anyway, he's not here. So you really can relax."

Verity popped into the bathroom to completely rid herself of her disguise and felt much better to be herself again. She emerged to find Karat coming to take her turn. "Stay in the suite. I'm going to check on the location of Hollingsworth's offices."

But as she left her rooms and Karat behind, she first went down the hall and knocked on a few doors —Anya's and Page's and Matt's—but no one seemed to be at home here, either. That left the lawyer, but it was a Saturday, so he was unlikely to be in. Still, as she had told Karat, it would be helpful to be sure how his offices were situated. She knew the address but had never visited. And if she was going to minimize any risk getting Karat to Hollingsworth, she'd have to be careful how they approached him.

An hour and a half later, it was a redhead with long, straight hair wearing sunglasses and four-inch heels who clicked her way through the lobby of the Whitaker building and boarded the express elevator for the fifty-fourth floor. Where the practice of Hollingsworth and Everett should've been, but showed no signs of actually being there.

Verity stalked her way down every corridor and investigated the entire floor but found nothing. She returned to the elevator, ready to go back and examine the directory in the lobby—but when an old man wheeling a yellow plastic pail and mop arrived with the elevator, it was too good an opportunity to pass up. She held the doors open for him and received a nod of thanks.

"Maybe you can help me?" Verity smiled at the janitor. "I was looking for Hollingsworth and Everett, but I must've gotten off on the wrong floor."

The old man shook his head without looking at her. "You got the right floor, alright, but they're not here anymore."

"You mean not in this building? I don't suppose you happen to know where they moved to?" Verity

Chapter 7

could always look it up in the phone book, but this would be faster. If he knew.

"They didn't move, they dissolved the practice. The young one went and joined one of the big firms on Wall Street. I heard the old guy retired—which is what I'd do if I could afford to."

Verity sighed and thanked the man, then waited for the next elevator down. If Hollingsworth had retired, she ought to find him at his house—as soon as she found out where that was—or out on the nearest golf course. She and Karat would stay at the Ngaio while she searched for him.

This was going to take up more time than Verity had anticipated. Hopefully she could find Hollingsworth soon and make Karat his problem before the baby arrived.

Chapter 8

Stranger in a Strange Land

September 9th, 1962 The Chihuahuan Desert

TURNER woke with a start, squeezed in on every side and encased in solid black. It was the sound of the wind, howling as it beat against the solid rock of the mountains, that reminded him of where he was. He didn't know how he'd gotten rest in such a compacted position, but now he was in a hurry to move. It was night, but he didn't know how long since the sun had fallen. What he knew was that he needed to cover as much distance as he could while it was still cool. *Help me get out of here.*

He tried to wiggle his fingers and toes, but most of his body was numb—he'd seized up in this awkward arrangement of his limbs and barely managed

Chapter 8

to wiggle his eyebrows. Since he'd used his knee as a pillow, even the right half of his face was frozen in place. His smile must've looked crooked.

Taking a deep breath, he focused his will to try to get his body to respond to the signals he knew his nerves were sending to his arms and legs. Gradually those nerves came alive—and he felt the pain. He clenched his teeth and ignored the protests running through his body and the throbbing in his head, and with care he gently eased each part as it woke up.

He shifted himself, bit by bit, toward the opening of the crevice. When at last he'd moved his head out into the night air, he could see the crisp light of the moon hanging low in the sky. It was still a little while longer before he had freed the rest of him and could check his watch. Almost midnight now.

Crawling away from the crevice, he then had to lie down and wait as a wave of pain surged through his body. Then as the agony abated, he had to relax and recover before he could slowly start stretching. He massaged his aching muscles and took his time standing up.

However much he had to take advantage of the nighttime cool, it wouldn't do him any good to try to walk anywhere until he was ready to do a proper job of it. Then he would see how far he could travel before the sun returned and he had to stop again. Assuming he could last that long.

First he turned to the south and examined what he could see of the peaks rising in front of him. He couldn't see a way through. Surely there had to be a pass of some kind somewhere, but he wasn't sure he wanted to cross to the other side. It would be better to head to the east, following the foothills and hoping they'd lead him where he wanted to go—which was civilization of any kind at this point.

Maybe daylight would reveal something that he couldn't see now, but if he wanted to survive he had to move. So with a soft sigh, he turned and started making his way east, and concentrated on watching where he walked to avoid falling on his face. Unless he found an oasis in the desert. He wouldn't complain about stumbling into a pool of water.

Unfortunately, finding a promising path for his feet meant he couldn't make as much progress as he would've hoped for—aside from navigating around those spiny little plants, he found the terrain forced him to veer up and down the slope as he went. *Not another night of this, please.*

For five hours he walked on, taking his time and taking short breaks to rest. When the morning sun rose in his eyes, he was grateful for the light and the warmth, but he knew that would change. He raised his hand to shield his eyes and turned his head slowly from side to side. And in the valley below, he saw a strange sight indeed.

Chapter 8

Almost a hundred yards ahead, at the foot of the slope, a small wooden shack stood in the shadow of a large wind turbine. Turner wondered if that could actually be civilization of a sort. He'd have to check it out.

At least it was early in the day, and if this didn't pan out, he still had plenty of time to search for water and shelter, but that shack looked a lot more inviting than another hole in the rock. It was a sign of life, anyway, and it gave him hope. *Thank You.*

Tired as he was from marching throughout the night, he was careful stepping down the slope as he made his way toward that oasis of a sort. He didn't despair when he got close enough to see there were no tire tracks from any kind of vehicle. It appeared to be abandoned, with no sign of life. Still, the first thing he did when he reached the door was knock.

Thinking he heard a rustling sound from inside, Turner rapped on the door again. That was followed by a blurry bellow, and then the door was swinging outward, and Turner had to jump back to avoid getting hit. He froze at the sight that greeted him.

"Strewth!" This exclamation became somewhat more comprehensible to Turner as he examined the skinny fellow squinting back at him from inside the shack. The man had a wild mane of bright-red hair and pasty white skin with freckles and wore a pair of blue denim overalls.

Turner shook his head to unscramble his brain. "I'm sorry if I surprised you, sir. But I'm afraid I'm lost. I'd hoped I was in Texas. Don't tell me I landed in Scotland?"

The man stood there with his mouth gaping for a long moment before barking something sounding almost like a laugh. "What'd you do—just drop out of the sky?"

"Something like that."

Shaking his head back and forth vigorously, the man looked incredulous. "I'll be blasted if someone like you could've ended up here if not by falling out of a plane."

"Someone like me?" As if the man standing before him could talk. "I'm surprised to find someone with your complexion out here in the middle of the desert—don't you get sunburned?"

"Don't go out in the sun to get burned. It's nicer at night anyway."

Turner blinked. It was a rather strange conversation to have in these circumstances. "Nice being a relative term in my opinion. I'm sure I would have appreciated it better if I'd had food and water." And somewhere more comfortable to sleep.

The man grunted. "My name's MacInnes, and I have water, at least—for a man who needs a drink in the desert."

"I'm Turner. And I won't refuse it."

Chapter 8

MacInnes stood and stared for a minute. "Suppose you've been walking all night?" It wasn't really a question.

"Like I said, I'm lost. I've come from that way." Turner pointed back the way he'd come. "I'm hoping to find a city, or town, or something. Along with that water, I'd appreciate it if you could give me the right direction to head in."

"A city? Why in the world would you want to go into one of those?" The man backed into the shack and motioned Turner to come in. "Difficult enough getting away from the darned things."

A cheap cot occupied the length of one wall—on the north side, underneath a window with mosquito netting instead of glass. On the other side sat a sink with a faucet next to a small counter on which sat an electric coffee pot. Against the far wall opposite the door was a cramped desk with a lamp on top. Next to that was a plain wooden chair. All the comforts of home.

MacInnes gestured for him to sit and turned to the sink with a coffee mug already in hand. Turner was grateful to sit down in the shade. He'd be even more glad to get that drink of water he'd been promised. His chances for survival—at least in the short term—were looking up.

"How did you end up here?" Hopefully the man would be happy to have someone to talk to. The opportunity couldn't come around that often. "I take it that windmill outside is what provides the energy to run the coffeepot and the lamp?"

"Aye. And to run the pump for the well." MacInnes filled the mug with water from the tap, handing it to Turner with a caution. "Drink slow, son, or you'll make yourself sick."

While Turner took his time slaking his thirst, his benefactor sat on the cot and told his story, in an abbreviated fashion.

"I'm an engineer. Dug the well, put the pump in, and set up the wind turbine. I built this place, with my own hands too. This is federal land, but I got a grant. It may not look like much, but I've got everything I need—shelter and water, coffee when I wake and light to read by, and plenty of room with no one crowding me."

Turner nodded. "And a great view you can enjoy in peace. But I didn't see any vehicles—how can you get food, or more books to read?"

"A couple times a year or so, someone will stop by with supplies. And if I really needed something, I could always just walk into town."

Hearing this, Turner asked the question he had been waiting to put to the man. "And how far away is this town? How do I get there?"

"Once you get on the other side of these mountains, it's only ten or fifteen miles to the road. Then

Chapter 8

it's another forty or fifty miles to the nearest town in either direction. You have to hope someone comes by to give you a lift, though, 'cause that's a long way to walk."

Turner tried to smile. After crossing the mountains and traveling ten miles beyond that, he didn't think he would be in any shape to walk further even if he wanted to—which he most definitely wouldn't. *Give me strength.*

"That's great. Can I get you to show me the best way through the mountains to get to this road? And maybe to find shelter, in case I can't make it over in one night?"

MacInnes nodded. "I can do better than that. I can take you up a ways to where there's a cool cave. It would give you a head start tonight, so you could reach the road before dawn. You don't want to wait out in the sun any longer than you have to."

Turner drank the last drop of water and handed the mug back to MacInnes. "I'd appreciate that. I want to thank you for the water too."

"Oh, there's plenty of water in the desert, if you know where to look. Take the agave plant, that little spiny thing you'll see all over the place. South of the border they sell the stuff you squeeze from its stalks as a sports drink."

And all along, Turner had been busy cursing the things for getting in his way. *Alright, the joke is on me. You'd provided what I needed, I just didn't recognize it.*

As soon as he was able to stop laughing, Turner slowly lifted himself from the chair, offering his new friend his hand. "Let's get going. I want you to get back here before the sun rises high enough to burn your Highland skin."

"Highland?" MacInnes snorted. "I come from North Carolina."

Turner shook his head. It took all sorts. While he saw the appeal of the man's lifestyle, it wasn't for him. Besides, he had a wife to get back to, even if it took him fifty years—but he could worry about that if and when he'd survived the desert.

"Wherever you're from, I'm grateful for all your help." *And Yours.* He felt better now that he knew where he was going. He wondered if he would actually make it, and what he'd find there if he did.

Chapter 9
Along for the Ride

September 24th, 1915 San Francisco

PAGE peeled back her glove and checked the date on her watch—precisely three years later than when she'd left, and she'd arrived in the exact same spot. At least her own Travel device was working properly. *But where in the world is Matt?*

She flipped to the locator screen, but once again there was no blip or bar to indicate the presence of any other Travelers in the present time. So the better question would be *when* Matt had gotten himself to. Not that she had any way to find out. She'd have to keep skipping three years at a hop until she found him. Even if that meant going a hundred years into the future. *But I don't have to rush about it.*

Stepping out from the seclusion of the copse of trees was difficult in the hobble skirt she had adopted in nineteen hundred twelve. She hoped women's fashions had gotten more practical during the three years she had skipped over, but she didn't expect it. Her next trip should take her to the end of the war, though, by which time things should've improved.

She began walking north through the park, and considered how unnecessary it was to Travel to and from some permanent base as Anya insisted. Page had simply gone for a stroll in the park and found a secluded spot. The scenery had changed so little in three years that the shift in reality had barely been noticeable. If only the trip ten years into the future had gone so smooth.

For now, she ought to focus on making the most of her time in nineteen hundred fifteen. It would be interesting to see what had changed. Margaret and Nancy would help her with what to look for, if they were still here, and Page couldn't imagine why they wouldn't be. But first she would go to the bank.

Hopefully getting some money from this year's trust stipend would be quicker than before, but she should get the process started. Waiting for approval would still likely give her plenty of time to get some research done while she was here.

With the tiny steps she had to take, across grass in her curved heels, it seemed to take forever to get

Chapter 9

to the north end of the park. By that time she wasn't about to take a packed cable car through the city. It wouldn't be necessary, thankfully, since her last visit to the bank had left her flush with cash.

So instead, Page bypassed the cable car station and went straight to where a line of cars had parked along the side of the road. Unfortunately they were all empty and unattended—except for one, where a youth sat on the running board and played jacks on the sidewalk.

She walked up to him and held out a dollar bill. "Young man, if you know where to find a cab, fetch the driver. Tell him I want to hire a car and the dollar is his if he'll take me where I want to go. And I'll give you a tip if you bring him quick."

The boy swept up his ball and jacks in a single smooth motion and stood. "This is a cab, miss, and it's mine. I'll not only take you where you want to go —for a dollar I'll drive you around all day."

Page squinted at the young scamp. Even if this boy had some connection to this car, it could not be his, and he certainly wasn't a cabbie. However, she was curious to see what he'd do. "Alright, then. It's a deal."

His eyes wide, the boy nodded and snatched the bill out of her hand, stuffing it into his pocket before offering her his hand to help her up into the back of the automobile. Once she was safely in her seat, he clambered up behind the wheel and started the engine. "Where'd you want to go first, my lady?"

"Cheeky boy. You haven't given me your name, and I'd like to know how old you are, if you're driving a car and supposed to be a cabbie."

"I'm Willim, miss, and I'm already twelve years old. Do you want to just sit here and talk, or do you want to tell me where to?"

"My name is Page, Willim. And I'd like to go to the American International State Bank in the financial district. That's—"

"I know where it is. On Montgomery. I tell you I know where everything is in this city."

With a jerk and a bounce, the car swerved suddenly into the street, barely missing a young couple walking along and cutting off another car. The boy seemed oblivious to it all. He certainly had a future as a cabbie—albeit possibly a very short one.

While he struggled with the gears and the clutch to get up and down the hills, Willim delivered her to the bank without getting in an accident. She wasn't sure what he might've left in their wake, and she did not want to know. He pulled up right in front of the building, and she slid out of the back seat and down to the ground before he made it around to help her. She was beginning to get used to these fool dresses, just in time to leave them behind. She wouldn't be missing them, even if they were elegantly charming.

Chapter 9

Page gave the boy a severe look. "I expect you to be here waiting when I come out. It may be a while. Do you have a book to read?"

He rolled his eyes at her. "A book? I've got my jacks."

Shaking her head, she turned and stepped into the bank. A clerk quickly summoned Mr. Pitt. And she gave thanks that banks didn't have a high turnover rate—it certainly made things convenient. She expected to meet many different bankers as it was, if she ended up having to go all the way to the twenty-first century to find Matt.

Page planned to take half of the yearly stipend every three years. She could build up her bank account as she advanced through the twentieth century, and hopefully she'd be prepared for the inevitable trouble Matt would involve her in—not to mention the expense of food and lodging and dresses.

Anya certainly wouldn't need any stipend funds from this century—she was only interested in Traveling farther into the future, toward home. Samantha's skimpy needs would barely make a dent in the trust the professor had established. There would be enough remaining for Matt if he were wandering in the twentieth century somewhere.

Matt was sufficiently clever to figure out how to use the professor's watch to access the trust funds if he needed them. She didn't know where or when he was, or what he might have to do to reach her—but he'd better be hard at work on that problem. *I miss him.* So he'd best not take too long to find her.

Page turned her attention to Mr. Pitt, who was approaching with the deference due a client with a substantial deposit. "Good morning, Miss Page. It's good to see you back again, safe and sound."

She'd told him she traveled a lot, quite truthfully, and apparently he worried. "I've come about this year's stipend—"

The banker held up his hand. "Of course. Now that we have a telephonic connection with the New York branch it will be much simpler than before. A short call to confirm your access and a day or two to process your request and the funds will be added to your account. Will that be satisfactory?"

Page nodded slowly. "I'll be staying in the city, so I may be back to make a withdrawal, but just taking care of the stipend will be sufficient for today."

"Of course." Already leading her back to his office, Mr. Pitt glanced over his shoulder at her. "And a young man left a message for you."

Page's pulse quickened. "A letter for me?" Matt had been with her when she'd received a communication across time from Sam—in the form of a letter left in a safe deposit box. "From whom?"

Mr. Pitt shook his head. "No letter. A Mr. Matt left only a verbal message to be passed on."

Chapter 9

Back in the banker's office, Page grabbed a pen and paper and jotted down her funds request along with the day's access code. She handed it over with a sigh. "So what's this message?"

"That he would meet you when you arrived back in town—but that if for some reason he wasn't here, he wanted you to wait for him. I am afraid that was the entirety of his message."

While the banker sat behind his desk and began placing a call to New York, Page thought about what Matt's message meant. He must've been in the relative past to have left it. But why hadn't he left her a letter to explain in detail what had happened to him and where he was? *And why isn't he here?*

Then she saw Mr. Pitt was already nodding and writing down the details of the transaction. He replaced the receiver and smiled at her. "Your access has been confirmed, and the money will be credited to your account by the end of the week. Will that be all?"

"Yes. Thank you, Mr. Pitt."

Striding out of his office and across the lobby to leave the bank, her mind stayed on Matt. They had tested the temporal tuner—which had worked properly—so Matt should know exactly where and when to find her. If he had taken the slow path from the past to reach her, he should be here now, or at least be showing up on her locator screen, but he wasn't.

Could he have been so foolish as to try Traveling to her coordinates with the professor's watch?

Back on the street, Page was glad that she didn't need to worry about tracking down a lost chauffeur. Willim was sitting on the running board, sulking.

He brightened, though, when he saw her. "This ground is no good for playing jacks. I expected it to take you a lot longer—I'm glad it didn't."

Smiling at the boy indulgently, she climbed into the back seat. "You can read anywhere, you know."

"Books are boring."

"I take it you've never tried Rudyard Kipling or Jack London. I doubt you'd find *them* boring."

She watched him scramble up behind the wheel and start the engine. Then she took Margaret's card from her reticule and passed it up to the boy. "Can you find this address alright?"

He rolled his eyes at her. "Nob Hill, and everyone knows where those ladies live."

Leaning back as the car rocketed into the street, Page turned her mind from Willim's driving back to the problem with Matt. If instead of taking the sure slow path to reach her he'd used the professor's device, he could have ended up anywhere in time and space. Then she realized that she hadn't asked Mr. Pitt when Matt had left that message, or how.

Supposing Matt had landed in Chickadee, at the right place but in the wrong time—he would've seen

Chapter 9

both when and where she had landed and would've started off across the country to meet her. He could have sent that message to the San Francisco branch ahead of him, knowing she'd go there. He might be rushing across the continent toward her right now.

It would explain why he'd asked her to wait if he wasn't there when she arrived—but it didn't explain why he wasn't showing up on her watch. She peeled back her glove and checked the locator app again to see there was still no blip or bar. A red bar ought to light up even if he was on the other side of the globe in the present time, but she knew better than to rely on that. From experience. She would have to trust Matt to do whatever he had to do to get to her—and if he got himself into trouble along the way, he was capable of taking care of himself, mostly. She would do her part by staying in the present.

That would be no hardship. She looked forward to seeing Margaret and Nancy again. During those two weeks she'd spent in nineteen hundred twelve, she'd called on the women three times to hear them talk about various courting couples. Though they'd gone on about other topics as well.

Page had also visited various restaurants where she'd been able to observe people dancing. Though without Matt there to help her, she'd had to content herself with watching and taking notes, when she'd rather have experienced the ritual first-hand.

Willim had struggled with the gears to make his way up the hill, but he'd finally managed—now they were turning past the gates and up the curving road leading to the elegant Georgian mansion that Nancy and Margaret called home. Soon Page would learn what they had been up to during these three years.

When they pulled up before the front entrance, Page alighted and turned back to Willim. "That side road leads to a coach house where you can park the car. And if you come to the back door, I'm sure they will feed you in the kitchen."

He grinned. "Yes, my lady."

Page walked up the marble steps and reached to lift the knocker, but the door opened before she was able to. Standing there was the Chinese butler she'd met previously. Except for his face, and a lingering accent, he could've been the perfect English butler—he certainly seemed as clever as the fictional Jeeves. Were he not gainfully employed, Page could see him becoming a criminal mastermind in San Francisco's underworld.

He essayed a slight bow at her. "Miss Page, I'm sure the Misses Margaret and Nancy will be pleased that you've come to visit after so long a time."

"You're looking well, Mr. Chiang. My chauffeur went to park in the coach house, and I told him he'd be welcomed in the kitchen. I hope that's alright."

"Certainly, miss. And you're too kind."

Chapter 9

He turned and she followed him down the main hall to a cozy room where Margaret and Nancy were enjoying their morning tea. Chiang announced her in ringing tones, though she was standing right behind him, waving at the two women.

Margaret smiled and nodded at an empty chair across from herself and Nancy. "Dear Page, where in the world have you been? It's been ages. Join us for tea, won't you?"

Nancy hurriedly stuffed the hunk of cake sitting on her fork into her mouth. She then leaped to her feet and scurried out of the room.

Page squinted at the empty space she'd left behind. "Is Nancy alright? I just got back into town, and I thought I'd stop by for a chat to catch up."

"She's alright, just excited. I think she wants to show you—" She broke off as Nancy bounded back into the room. "Her new hat."

Nancy held it out for a moment to let Page get a good look at the thing before donning it and affecting a pose. "Well?"

Page stared for a moment, trying to think what to say. Atop the wide, floppy brim, a vast multitude of long, brown-and-white striped feathers extended forth from a dark mass in all directions. "Looks like a turkey imploded on top of your head."

Nancy blinked, and Margaret kept a blank look on her face as she spoke. "You have a wicked sense of humor, Page. We should be quite appalled. *You* don't even wear a hat."

Nancy nodded. "After the beautiful one we got for you, I'd hoped you would've learned to appreciate a really fine hat."

Shaking her head, Page turned the subject away from hats—she'd made her feelings known. "Now, why don't you tell me what you two have been up to while I've been gone. I don't suppose you have met any decent men?"

Nancy snorted. "Are there such creatures?"

Margaret smiled as her companion sat down to take another slice of cake. "Plenty of nice men have tried to court us—for our money, of course—and we have enjoyed ourselves immensely. But why would we give up our independence to take on the burden of a husband?"

Page sighed. "That thinking makes sense, until you fall in love. Then you'll find yourself making the most ridiculous sacrifices."

Obviously bristling, Nancy objected. "Never. I shouldn't have to sacrifice anything—should I want a man in my life."

Margaret lifted one side of her mouth, and Page suspected she had a better understanding of the realities of life. "As we gain more legal rights, such as suffrage, we can make more decisions for ourselves, but love…"

Chapter 9

Page was confused. "I thought you already had the right to vote. The last time I was here, you spent a lot of time arguing about which of the three presidential candidates you wanted to vote for. And you were involved in local politics, weren't you?"

"Of course we've had the vote in California for a long time now—we're more enlightened here in the West. Every woman in the country should have that right, but we're facing a lot of resistance and downright hostility. They're afraid of us."

"Who? Men?"

Margaret shook her head. "Just the ones frightened we'll pass temperance laws—and the big business interests who make money from alcohol."

Page was interested in spite of herself. "Would you? Make drinking illegal?"

"There are already temperance laws in many areas, but it should be left to local communities to decide. Anyway, it doesn't make sense to try to outlaw alcohol nationally when most of the opposition is in the big urban areas."

Nancy interjected. "Like New York City. We'll probably see another riot."

"A riot? What are you talking about? And why New York instead of San Francisco?"

"I'm talking about the riot when we marched in D.C. It only helps our cause when they turn to violence to try and shut us up."

Margaret waved Nancy back into the seat she'd leapt out of. "Next month we're going to march for women's suffrage in New York City. We hope to rally support and put pressure on politicians to pass it in the state legislature."

Page smiled. She knew they would succeed, but that it would take longer than they'd like. "The war may get in the way of anything happening too fast."

"You mean the European War? America will be staying out of that nonsense."

"Well..." Page waited while Nancy poured her a cup of tea and decided to leave the subject of World War I alone. "You said '*we're* going to march'—does that mean you and Nancy are going to New York?"

Margaret nodded vigorously. "Since we've got the time and money, we have a responsibility to get involved. We're organizing the contingent to represent the state of California."

A train of thought started in Page's mind. "And when exactly is this protest happening?"

"Not a protest, a parade. We've been promised the protection of the New York City Police Department, so even if some people try to make trouble, it should be perfectly safe. Why don't you come along with us? The march isn't for a month yet, but we'll be leaving for New York in three weeks."

Page processed the possibilities quickly. If Matt hadn't arrived by the time three weeks had passed,

Chapter 9

he could be in more trouble than he could handle on his own. He might even be in New York City, and if not—he could find her there as well as anywhere.

She temporized. "I'd love to go with you, but I don't know about my future plans yet. If I'm able to go, I will. And I can arrange my own travel and accommodations, so you can plan without me."

Nancy didn't seem satisfied, but Margaret nodded in acceptance, so Page settled back to enjoy her tea and see if she could get some news of the social scene out of these two activists. Later, she'd need to find a bookstore and get Willim something to read—but before that, a nice hotel suite to stay at for three weeks. Assuming Matt didn't show up sooner than that.

And he should show up soon. If he didn't, Page would have to work hard at not wondering what difficulties he might be experiencing.

Chapter 10
Parade Rout(e)

October 23rd, 1915 Midtown Manhattan

MATT directed his bags to the hotel, then left Penn Station cross and exhausted from the trip across the continent. It wasn't the train—the views, the berth, and even the food had been first class. It was worry about Page that had left its mark. He'd set off after her across the country, but various delays had made him late—she had already been in New York at least a week. If she were still here.

Exiting onto Thirty-second Street, he surveyed the crowds, looking for Page even though he had no expectation he might happen to run into her, not in the middle of Manhattan—but he had to hope she'd be here somewhere, so he kept his eyes open.

Chapter 10

The real reason he was upset, of course, was the confounded watch—or rather how he was having to learn how it worked the hard way.

Two weeks after his arrival in nineteen hundred twelve, Matt had kept his eye on the temporal tuner and seen that Page had Traveled three years into the future, landing at nine thirty on September twenty-fourth in nineteen fifteen, and in San Francisco. He had even written down the latitude and longitude of the location, which placed her in or around Golden Gate Park. According to the watch.

Trying to Travel to that point in space and time would've been too risky using the professor's faulty device. But Matt had presumed all he had to do was wait three years, then show up in the general area at the time she'd be arriving and use the regular tracking function to find her. A few weeks later he'd happened to check the temporal tuner and seen that by the middle of October, nineteen fifteen, Page would be in New York City.

Matt reflected on this puzzle while walking east toward Broadway, a part of his brain still searching for Page among the throngs. At the time, he had assumed he would reunite with her in nineteen fifteen in San Francisco—that they would travel together to New York. It hadn't worked out that way.

He was glad that he had quit checking the temporal tuner, worried that having known where Page would be in the future had somehow fixed the fact of it in reality, like collapsing a quantum wave—a mistake he wouldn't want to repeat.

Those three years waiting in San Francisco had given Matt plenty of opportunity to study the watch itself and its programming. He'd also had the time to review all he knew about time-travel theory. But it was in practice that the rubber met the road, and when Matt had gone to Golden Gate Park the morning of September twenty-fourth, then tried tracking Page with the locator app, she hadn't appeared. After nine thirty, when he knew she must have arrived there somewhere, he hadn't seen any blip or bar to guide him. So he'd resorted to running through the park looking for her. He had searched for hours before giving up. Then he'd gone to the bank.

Matt still ground his teeth when he recalled that conversation with Mr. Pitt. Yes, Miss Page had visited the bank that morning, but the lady had left already. No, Mr. Pitt didn't know where he could find her, but he believed she was still in the city. He *had* given her Matt's message, but, no, she had not waited or left any note for him.

Frustrated with the banker's attitude and Page's not having waited for him, or at least left a message saying where she could be found, Matt had searched through shops all over town, as well as clubs, hotels, and restaurants. And all to no avail. So after a cou-

Chapter 10

ple of weeks scouring the city in vain, and knowing that Page would soon wind up in New York City, he had taken the train across the continent. But if she was still here somewhere, how would he be able to find her when he hadn't been able to in California?

Without the watch able to provide even a direction, he had little hope of finding Page amongst the masses. But he knew he'd be searching for her anyway. His best hope was that the manager at the main branch here would be more helpful than Mr. Pitt in San Francisco. Surely Page would need to withdraw some cash while she was in New York City. She may have already. Unfortunately, Matt had arrived on a Saturday and would now have to wait until Monday to find out.

At the intersection with Broadway, Matt divided his mind between crossing safely and continuing to look for Page. He knew he'd recognize her, even at a distance, if once he saw her. He looked at faces in the crowd and the backs of heads and silhouettes seen through shop windows as he walked on toward Fifth Avenue. He also hoped that if he could just see her, even from far away, it would short out the time differential between them.

Otherwise, if he searched and searched and still couldn't find her, he'd have to risk Traveling. He'd stopped checking the temporal tuner out of concern that seeing where she would be in his relative future

Parade Rout(e)

might somehow keep them separated. If he looked at it again, it would be to find the right coordinates to set for Traveling. But if he did that, where in time and space might he actually end up? Even attempting to go just a couple weeks into the future might only take him further from Page.

Until he'd discovered what went wrong with the initial test trip with the master Travel device, trying again would be an act of desperation.

With his mental functions occupied on multiple levels, it took Matt a while to realize he had stopped behind a large crowd waiting at the Fifth Avenue intersection, and never moved on. He looked up and down the street and saw he was stuck at the back of a solid mass of people standing six to twelve deep on both sides. As far as the eye could see. *It's too early for Macy's Thanksgiving Day Parade.* That tradition probably hadn't even started yet.

Whatever parade might be coming, Matt wasn't going to be crossing Fifth Avenue anytime soon. He should probably start searching the shops. What he did, though, was use his height to scan the crowd on either side of the street. Passing over the policemen in their uniforms holding back the throngs, he tried to pick out the redheads among the watchers lining the sidewalks.

He could swiftly dismiss them all one by one because Page always wore the same hairstyle. He had

Chapter 10

asked her about that, and she'd explained that she'd found the cut that looked best on her, so she wasn't about to change it. He'd teased her, telling her that too much variety with her clothes had overwhelmed her senses. But he'd had to admit she never looked anything but gorgeous.

Eventually he'd need to check in at the hotel, so he started working his way slowly along the back of the crowds, continuing to hunt for Page as he went. As he did, he met the head of the parade advancing from the opposite direction. Women marching with a banner proclaiming the need for the right to vote—seeing that, Matt was glad for the heavy police presence. In addition to the men who were standing out in front of the crowd, a number of mounted officers patrolled between them and the marchers.

He considered going into some of the stores as he passed by, but the staff were probably all watching the parade. Once he'd refreshed himself at the hotel, he could go out again, searching. By then the parade should be over.

Swiveling his head from side to side, he spotted four women carrying a stretcher loaded with ballot boxes and wondered which shops would be the best prospects for finding Page. She did tend to make an impression, so if he described her, the saleswomen should remember. The question was whether Page had made purchases or not—and left an address for deliveries if she had. And if so, whether or not Matt could get that information. The odds were slim he'd run into Page herself, whichever shop he happened to try.

He doubted Macy's was upscale enough for her. *Bergdorf Goodman?* He was waffling over whether to try there first when something in the back of his brain alerted him to something he'd noticed but not paid attention to, the mood of the men around him. He had wandered behind a large group of laborers—men who had clearly been drinking heavily already, despite the early hour.

From their grumbling, they weren't supporters. Roughly dressed and unwashed, the beer fumes exuded from their clothes as well as their breath. And they sounded aggressive and eager to begin making trouble.

"Look at that one, bold as brass and the hair to match with her nose in the air."

Matt's mind picked that one comment out from the mix and his eyes flew over the crowd to the people marching. And like iron filings drawn to a powerful magnet, they locked on Page. Wearing a modern hat and a fashionable outfit of the time—a long, bright green dress with a short tan tunic—she stood out from her fellow suffragettes, all wearing white.

She was walking with the California contingent. Which made sense—she must have hooked up with

Chapter 10

some activists in San Francisco, then accompanied them here. Rather than wait for him.

As she drew closer, Page must have sensed him there, because she suddenly turned her head to look directly at where he was standing. Glad for his long legs putting his head above the throng, Matt waved at her. And grinned like a maniac.

One of the men around him turned and glared. "Hey, pal. You friends with one of these broads?"

The tone was hostile, and Matt glanced around to see how close the nearest policeman was while he replied. "Those are ladies you're talking about, and yes. One of them is a friend of mine."

The belligerent man pushed against him. "Well your friend ain't no lady if she wants the vote."

Some of his friends had turned around to back him up, and one added in an aggrieved tone, "They'll turn the whole country dry if we let 'em."

The first man nodded while keeping his glare on Matt. "But we won't let 'em, will we?"

Seeing the way these men were behaving, Matt could understand why a lot of people had believed Prohibition would be a good idea. It didn't work out that well in the end, but clearly it had been tried for a reason. *A good reason.*

Out of the corner of his eye, he could just make out Page waving at him, but he could not see the expression on her face. Hopefully it was joy at his hav-

Parade Rout(e)

ing found her, even if it was by accident. He imagined her crystal blue eyes lighting up.

Angry lout number one then shoved his fist into Matt's shoulder, pushing that side of him backward as he pivoted on an axis. Figuring it would be much better to draw these troublemakers toward himself and away from the marchers, he shifted his feet and lifted his knee as the man shoved. Angry lout number one dropped to the ground, moaning in pain.

Even in the crush of the crowd, this hadn't gone unnoticed by the man's irate compatriots. A highly inebriated fellow raised his fist, presumably prelude to trying to hit Matt—which didn't go unnoticed by a nearby policeman, who blew his whistle. But everything was already escalating out of control at that point.

Matt shifted his feet and raised his hands to deflect the assailant's fist and send it crashing into another would-be attacker's face. As he dodged out of the way of a third man, he saw Page running toward him. But she wouldn't be able to reach him between the now rioting crowd and the policemen who were converging on the scene to quell the mob. Matt was amused to find himself right in the middle of it all.

One of those angry louts grabbed him, and Matt barely avoided a headbutt—then he saw the look of horror on Page's face, over the few dozen people between them. But her expression changed to a smile

Chapter 10

as she pulled something out of her purse. Her Travel device. And Matt realized she was going to try to rescue him, and how.

As he slipped past a flying fist and dropped another assailant, it hit him why what she was going to try might not work—what the potential result could be. He tried to shout to her over the increasing din. "No, Page. Wait!"

He caught the flash of doubt in her face just before she pushed a button on the watch and vanished right in front of everyone. Not that anyone noticed. Then someone's fist connected with his jaw, sending him reeling backwards. Someone else knocked into him from behind, and he was sailing right back into the fray, sliding past another incoming punch—and driving his own fist up through that one's jaw. Matt stepped behind the man, lifting with his hip to send him careening to the ground. *I've lost her again.*

He needed to get out of this mess and away, so he could think what he'd do next. She had probably Traveled another three years into the future. But he couldn't be sure. And if he checked to see—

Hands grabbed at him from both sides. He saw police diving into the melee and laying about themselves with their truncheons. As they were hauling him away, one of the policemen holding him cuffed his hands in front of him—then he and his attackers were being dragged off to the boos and hisses of the crowd. The police stuffed all of the combatants into a waiting paddy wagon. Including Matt, of course.

Given their state of inebriation and general ragged condition, he wouldn't have been worried about sharing the back of the truck with his attackers even if a couple of cops hadn't climbed in with them. He *was* worried about Page. Whenever or wherever she had Traveled to, she might be in trouble. And Matt was not going to wait around for three more years—not when he'd gotten so close to her. Maybe it had been enough to short out the time differential so the locator app could track her again. He'd have to take the risk regardless.

The vehicle lurched off down the street, and he had to steady himself against the drunk beside him—then Matt kept glancing out a little window in the door to see where they were going. He would have to wait for the right timing.

Casually he lifted the cuff of his shirtsleeve and flipped the screen of his watch over to the temporal tuner. Page *had* Traveled three years into the future exactly, arriving at the same latitude and longitude she had left from. Matt flipped over to the Traveling app and set the watch for that same three years forward. Now he was prepared to leave. But he had to Travel soon, while he'd still land physically close to where Page had arrived. Assuming that the professor's device would work the way Matt had surmised

Chapter 10

it should. He only needed to wait for a calm mind—and a lack of bumps in the road. All he needed was to hit the wrong button by mistake and land himself in the Middle Ages.

He saw they were traveling down Thirty-fourth Street, and when the paddy wagon stopped behind a line of other vehicles at the busy Broadway intersection, Matt prepared to push the right buttons. Facing his fellow prisoners, he grinned at them. "I take it you guys have heard of Harry Houdini, right?"

Then he Traveled away, leaving who knew what confusion in his wake.

Chapter 11
Nye on the Street

June 22nd, 2003 Midtown Manhattan

NYE swiveled her head in every direction to make sure she was getting it all, not just the buildings but the people as well. The more raw data she collected for analyzing, the better the results she would get—the problem with people was knowing what to look for. She was collecting plenty of information about these twenty-first century denizens, but Nye wasn't sure where or how to start evaluating what she had. At least with the buildings, she knew what she wanted to know.

She barely had the time to do her proper work—she wouldn't have the chance to organize a study of New Yorkers too. The city itself was already almost

Chapter 11

too much for her. The overview of the five boroughs and the city's layout—the general information she'd collected at the start—it made her task seem gargantuan. All the days she'd spent in in-depth examination only made the work seem much more daunting. Studying this city's dead remains now seemed simple in comparison.

Nye was still surveying Midtown after three and a half summers. She had tried to talk to Anya about staying there year-round, but the two times her leader had come to visit, ostensibly to see how Nye was doing, the woman had been far too busy with some business of her own to have a proper discussion. So Nye just kept on doing what she could, with her resolve hardening to tackle Anya at some point.

Crossing from block to block, Nye passed from a poor section to an upscale area and back to one less prosperous without any real demarcations between them. And all in the same so-called neighborhood. Shaking her head, she considered the lack of properly defined and labeled boundaries between these communities. Just in this one part of one borough, there were so many different and distinctive neighborhoods it was hard to keep track.

Nye could make dividing lines of her own when the time came, but she would worry about that after she'd finished documenting these areas. She ought to focus on doing that first.

Evaluating the run-down old apartment buildings around her, that dilapidated repair shop down the street, and the dingy auto garage beside it, Nye nodded to herself. She appreciated how these structures created and defined a certain atmosphere specific to this neighborhood. Then she fixed on one of the big waste receptacles sitting on the sidewalk. In addition to the buildings, Nye sometimes inspected the contents of these trash containers—which gave her further insight into the character of the community.

There was an analysis she knew she intended to run. She would see how closely the composition of a community's garbage compared with the neighborhood itself. Were the distinctions between communities apparent in their trash?

Walking up to the container she had picked out, Nye reached into the opening and began pulling out one item after another to set on top of the lid.

She was engaged in this methodical work when an older woman wearing variegated layers of dress and pushing a packed shopping cart came trundling over. "Hey, that's *my* can. Get away. Go find your own gold mine."

Nye blinked until she realized what the woman was talking about. "You're welcome to the contents of the container, mam. I was only looking inside to see what's there. But I haven't found any gold yet."

Chapter 11

Scratching the woolen cap on her head, the old woman scrutinized Nye for a long moment. "Never found gold myself, but I've gotten some real treasures from this one." She laughed. "Maybe I'll find gold someday, though."

Nye stepped back from the can. "Since I'm just interested in knowing what's in there, I'd appreciate it if you'd allow me to watch you search to see what you find." That would give her the opportunity not only to document the container's contents, but also the habits of the people in this community.

But the woman squinted at her. "You want me to do all the work? And then I suppose if I find anything really good, you'll just take it from me?" She shook her head, then brushed aside the stringy gray hair falling across her eyes. "Hey, I know you."

Blinking to activate the facial recognition function of her glasses, Nye was soon watching a video playback of the time this woman had come into her field of vision. Back in the summer of two thousand, when Nye had spent a short time being evaluated at a behavioral health hospital, this old lady had been on the same ward.

Nye nodded at her. "You've got a good memory. I don't think we were ever properly introduced."

The woman smiled to reveal a mouth missing a lot of teeth. "I don't suppose we were. I'm Jeannie, by the way, and I'm surprised they let you go."

"My name is Nye. But they released you—" Obviously, because here the woman was, searching the trash cans just like Nye. "So I'm not sure why you'd be surprised to see me."

Jeannie just shook her head. "You looked like a crazy person to me, but then I'm no doctor. Every now and then these nice cops take me to the hospital, but only 'cause they want me to get some good grub and a roof over my head for a while. Of course, the drugs are horrible, but you get to meet new people. Like you."

"They take you to a mental hospital to feed you and give you drugs you don't need or want? It certainly doesn't sound very efficient. Why not a shelter or something?"

"It's 'cause of the voices I hear. The doctors try to prove I'm crazy, but they can't, so then they have to let me go. Sometimes I'll string them along for a while—if I'm not ready to leave."

"But you're not crazy?"

"If I was crazy, the voices wouldn't be telling me things that are true. Like where I'd seen you before. I'm the only one who can hear them, though, so the doctors have a difficult time believing."

Nye nodded. "I see. I get information through my glasses, but no one else can see it." She doubted it would do any good to try explaining their isomorphic graphics display technology to Jeannie. "Don't

Chapter 11

you think it would be better to keep the voices all to yourself, though? If people wouldn't believe?" That was what Nye did. That was why it was still inexplicable to her why the cops had taken her in for a psychiatric evaluation.

Jeannie laughed. "That's their problem. And if it wasn't the voices, they'd find something else they wanted to shrink inside my head."

"I suppose it doesn't matter. As long as they let us go, and they did." Although they apparently kept reeling Jeannie back in.

With a snort, Jeannie returned to her trash can, taking its lid off entirely and sorting quickly and efficiently through the contents. Nye was impressed. She had moved close enough to lean over and watch the entire process, and since it was all being recorded she could study the video later, at her leisure.

Jeannie took a couple items and stuffed them in her cart before throwing the trash back in and turning to smile at Nye. "I bet you're hungry. There's a good place for lunch just a couple of blocks away. It attracts a good crowd, too."

"Alright. I am getting hungry." She'd have been taking a lunch break about now anyway. She would likely learn more by accompanying Jeannie and observing her interactions with the locals than by just sitting inside some pizza parlor watching people as they ate. "Lead the way."

Following her new friend, Nye herself became a subject of observation by the natives. They must've known there was a question about Jeannie's mental health, and Nye's connection with the woman likely was a topic of speculation for them.

Looking at the various signs on the buildings as they strolled down the street, Nye ventured a question. "I like the way you know where you are here—'Kips Bay this, and Kips Bay that'—but why doesn't someone just put up signs at the boundaries?"

"What would be the point of that?"

Soon Jeannie had brought them both to the entrance to a dull, nondescript building with a faded, illegible sign. Next door to it stood a modern high-rise apartment building.

"This must be a really exclusive place."

Jeannie laughed. "Sure is. We're the only kind of people who can eat here." She pushed on in, and Nye followed.

Inside, rows of plastic-topped tables lined with rusting, gray, metal folding chairs ran across a vast space. A startling array of people sat at those tables, eating and chatting. Along the back wall, a few folks wearing white aprons stood behind a table draped with a heavy white cloth and served their customers soup out of giant pots, slices of bread, and even cups of coffee. Of course there was a very long line. "This looks good, Jeannie."

Chapter 11

They joined the back of the queue, and Jeannie patted the shoulder of a bald man standing with his back to her. "Hey, Bernie. I brought someone new. Meet Nye."

Bernie turned and smiled wide at both of them. Then he cast a critical eye over Nye. "You don't look like you belong here. You homeless?"

Nye smiled back. "I suppose that depends how you look at it. I feel at home wherever I am."

He scratched his cheek and considered this. "I like to think that way myself."

When they got to the head of the line, they took bright plastic trays from a huge pile and stopped in front of the person ladling out generous portions of cabbage soup into wide, shallow bowls before placing them onto people's trays.

Nye grinned at the woman. "Cabbage soup is a favorite of mine. Delicious *and* nutritious."

Another woman placed a couple slices of bread onto Nye's tray, and a man farther down poured her coffee into a Styrofoam cup. Then Nye joined Jeannie and Bernie at an empty table in the middle of the room.

Jeannie spoke low. "Those volunteers are nice, aren't they?"

"They're volunteers? Do you suppose they'd let me do that?"

"Why would you want to?"

Nye cocked her head at her new friend. "Well, if I'm going to be coming here to eat anyway..." And it was conveniently located for the zone she was currently researching. "Then why wouldn't I help out?" She thought it might also help her understand these people better.

Bernie shook his head and turned to the man on his other side. "You should hear this, George. New girl wants to volunteer here herself."

But the young man who was apparently named George quickly turned away from them, keeping his face down close to his bowl as he ate.

Bernie blushed and turned back to the women. "I guess George is shy. He's new too. You're a good looking girl, Nye. But he's a handsome young man, so I don't know why he should be so shy."

Nye began blinking furiously. She reviewed the video her glasses had been recording since she had entered and isolated George's face, then started the multi-layered analysis for finding various patterns. When the results displayed on her lenses a few moments later, Nye understood why young George was acting so shy around her.

Chapter 12

I Have to Do Something

June 30th, 2003 Midtown Manhattan

ANYA's appearance startled the secretary who was sitting at the reception desk on the forty-ninth floor —the same lobby Anya had just stepped into, three years in the past. The woman who'd been filing her nails and looked up to see Anya standing where nobody had existed a moment ago gave a little yelp before recovering herself.

"Oh, I hadn't heard the elevator. What can I do for you?"

Anya shook her head and reached behind her to hit the call button for an elevator going down. "I got off on the wrong floor. Sorry." No need to mention that she'd gotten off three years ago.

Turning to face the elevator doors and wait, Anya took the opportunity to check the locator app on her watch and was relieved to see only a red bar indicating the closest Travel device lay to the east, not a blip showing someone close on her heels. The device to the east was probably Nye. Still, if Anya had taken her pursuer along with her back to twenty-oh-three, the spatial dislocation would likely place him outside of her immediate range. But she did not see how he could have been in range to Travel with her at all.

No, she must've managed to leave the man with those cold, hard eyes and Kirin's watch three years in the past. It was all over now. Her mission to save the professor had been a complete failure. She had not even been able to bring the man who had struck and killed him to justice. Rather, Anya had run and now had to count escaping from that same man as a triumph—it was her only success. There was nothing left to do but go home.

She heard the ding of the elevator and waited as the doors opened before stepping into the car with a weary sigh. She shuffled to the rear, then leaned up against the railing. They stopped at two more floors to let on more passengers before dropping down to the ground level.

The doors opened to the lobby, and she let everyone else surge out ahead of her and followed with

Chapter 12

a tired tread. *I think I'll call Ralph to come and pick me up.* It would be easier than taking the train.

But Anya found her way blocked—by throngs of people who were being held back from the middle of the lobby by a couple of security guards. She heard plenty of murmuring and complaining, but nothing to explain what the problem was. Not until a guard had grown exasperated with everyone pushing forward and snapped out his own protest.

"Look—you all have to stay away from the body. You can't leave the building before the cops come to take control of the scene anyway, so why not return to your offices, or go to the café on the second floor? You're all going to be here for a while."

Anya had a sinking feeling in her stomach. She checked her watch again, and this time there was a blip almost in the center of the locator screen—right on the other side of these people.

Pushing her way through those ahead of her until she could see what everyone was staring at, what she saw looked like the man who had been pursuing her. It was hard to tell for sure, because he was still many meters away and lying in a heap on the lobby floor, and definitely dead. But the Travel device on his wrist had not been destroyed, or he wouldn't be showing up as a blip on hers.

Despite her best efforts, she must have Traveled this unknown watchbearer along with her. She had been so sure she'd put enough distance between the man and herself, she hadn't even bothered to check her locator screen before she left two thousand.

At least now she realized why none of the others had met this mysterious man back in the past. Anya herself had brought him three years forward to his death.

The man must have gotten onto one of the other express elevators just after her to have been so near that he'd been caught up in the field she had generated. And when she'd left two thousand, he must've still been soaring upward, and retained his momentum into two thousand three. The spatial separation must have materialized him in the lobby. And then his momentum would've propelled him up in the air before gravity brought him back down to the marble floor. At least he hadn't hurt anyone else in his fall. And Anya needn't worry about him anymore.

What Anya *was* concerned about was that watch of Kirin's on his wrist. She couldn't get close enough to his body to remove the device. And since she had depleted the charge on both batteries, Traveling his corpse away was out. Even if that would accomplish anything other than moving the watch farther from her and making it more difficult to retrieve.

Now the police were coming, and Anya thought she'd better leave the lobby before they showed up. Since she couldn't exit the building, she pushed her

Chapter 12

way back through the crowd and joined the handful of others who were waiting for the elevator. *Again.* She needed to figure out where she was going.

That café on the second floor that the guard had mentioned sounded appealing, as Anya was starting to feel peckish. But she had a more serious problem on her hands—what to do about that watch. Maybe she should've tried to deal with that in the past, instead of running, but now she had an opportunity to do something. If only she could think how.

Of course, following her own counsel up to this point hadn't worked out too well. That thought reminded Anya of the reason she'd had to be familiar with this building to begin with—Mr. Hollingsworth had his office on the fifty-fourth floor. Maybe it was time she consulted with her lawyer.

Anya got on one of the slower elevators without thinking, and it seemed to stop at almost every floor on its way up. That was good for her stomach—but bad for her brain, because she had plenty of time to review all the mistakes she had made this morning, and there were plenty. While she had tried to think through every eventuality and prepare for anything, it hadn't been enough.

She'd exercised bad judgment up and down the line, but her first and most egregious error had been trying to save the professor. She didn't know if she had really been the cause of the accident, or if he'd

I Have to Do Something

have died anyway, but the professor had warned her not to try to change history—and yet Anya had stubbornly gone ahead with her reckless plan. The only difference she could see she had made was to Travel the man who had hit and killed John back to the future. And even that wasn't to her credit—she hadn't been aware of what she was doing. Providence had used her reckless behavior to execute justice.

The constant dinging of the elevator kept interrupting her thoughts, and she tried to ignore it. She almost missed it then when the car finally arrived at the fifty-fourth floor, and Anya had to scramble out before the doors closed. Instead of a lobby, only the blank purple wall met people coming off the elevator, and a corridor stretching in either direction.

Anya turned right and strode down the hallway until she arrived at the large oak door with a gilded plaque proclaiming 'Hollingsworth and Everett, esquires' in tasteful elegance. She knocked first, then turned the knob and walked into the outer office.

The russet-haired woman seated behind the reception desk was middle-aged and sturdy, reminding Anya of herself, except for the color of her hair, and occupied on the phone. Anya nodded to the receptionist and removed herself to the far side of the room and waited. Too anxious to sit down, she just stood and stared at one of the abstract paintings on the wall.

Chapter 12

After a while she heard the click of the receiver being replaced and Ms. Cooper's voice behind her.

"How are you this morning, Anya?"

Turning around, Anya smiled at her. "I'm sorry I don't have an appointment, but this problem came up rather suddenly—and I happened to be nearby. I thought if I stopped by there might be a chance you could find a way to squeeze me in for brief chat with him."

The secretary smiled. "For you, Ms. Walker, I'm sure he'll manage something. He has another client with him right now, though, so it might be a bit of a wait."

"I don't mind." She would have to wait anyway, somewhere doing something. "I'm not in any rush." If only that had been true earlier, maybe Anya could have avoided the mess she was in now.

Turning around again, she forced herself to sit down in one of the plush armchairs lined up against the wall. And had nothing to do other than watch to see when Mr. Hollingsworth's client left, or observe Ms. Cooper, who had already gone back to her work. She and the lawyer would make a good match. Anya wondered why he'd never married—which was none of her business, only her mind trying to distract her from other thoughts. Less pleasant ones.

If she hadn't gone back to try to save the professor, would he have died? Now that she'd had some experience traveling through time, she realized that the professor's disorientation right before the accident was not a natural reaction for a seasoned Traveler like John. It had been her dual appearance that must have confused him.

She also had to acknowledge that if she had not gone back in time, trying to change things, that sinister watchbearer wouldn't have had anyone to lead him to the spot. Maybe some other driver would've hit the professor, even if he hadn't been disoriented by Anya's actions, but she'd never know.

She forced herself to confront her own timidity. Alright, trying to save the professor had been a mistake—but one she may have needed to make. It certainly had given her an opportunity—to take care of several things which she hadn't known needed to be dealt with, or hadn't imagined she would ever have the chance to address.

One of those issues was the question of the person who'd hit and killed the professor. At the time she'd just assumed it to be an accident, and that the authorities would take care of everything. And then the police had tried to pin his death on her—an allegation she now knew had more behind it than those detectives could've known. And somehow in all that mess, no one had ever been brought to account. Until now. She had discovered the truth and inadvertently delivered some justice.

Chapter 12

Then also, Anya believed she'd discovered what had happened to Kirin's missing watch—she'd been given a chance to retrieve the advanced future technology from someone who certainly shouldn't have been in possession of it. And blew it.

Throughout it all, Anya had been a coward. She had balked at throwing herself into traffic to try to save the professor like she'd planned. She'd chased that hit-and-run driver, but only until she'd realized he was a danger to her. And then, instead of trying to find some way to deal with him and get the watch back, she'd just run away. When she was supposed to be a leader.

Get a grip on yourself. She *was* a leader, so she needed to start acting like one. One of their Travel devices needed to be retrieved, and Anya would just have to find a way to get it back.

Ms. Cooper calling her name brought Anya out of her self-examination. "Mr. Hollingsworth is free for a few minutes now. Just go right on back. You know the way."

Anya stood and smoothed her skirt. She smiled at the secretary and straightened her spine. Marching over to the door beyond Ms. Cooper's desk, Anya turned the knob and walked down the short corridor to the lawyer's spacious corner office.

His door stood open, and he'd risen to stand behind his desk. He nodded and smiled in his genteel

I Have to Do Something

way. "It's good to see you again, Miss Walker, even if you've gotten yourself into some more trouble."

Anya stepped in and then stopped, as always, to appreciate the breathtaking view of the city out the wall of windows that took up one side of the office. "I'm not sure if that's supposed to be a compliment or not, Mr. Hollingsworth."

He combed his finger down his salt-and-pepper mustache and grinned. "You should take it as one—but maybe it's one of your colleagues who's in trouble this time?"

She smiled as she sat down in one of the leather chairs facing his desk. Waiting until he'd sat down himself, Anya shook her head. "It's me. At least I'm the one who needs your help, but it's not really trouble. Just a rather thorny problem."

"As long as you remember my advice to not tell me more than I ought to know."

"Of course." He'd told Anya she shouldn't ever lie to him, but that sometimes there were things he was better off not knowing. "And you'll let me know what it is you need from me."

"Alright, then. What's this problem, and how is it you think I can help?"

"If you haven't heard already, you will soon—a man died not long ago in the lobby of this building. When I was down there, I heard the police had been called and were on their way."

Chapter 12

"I hadn't heard. And the police have surely arrived by now. Are they your problem?"

Anya shook her head. "I don't think so. Not directly. But the dead man had something in his possession that did not belong to him, and I need to get it. I doubt the police will just give it to me."

Mr. Hollingsworth nodded. "I see. Well, if it's become a police investigation, I'm afraid that they'll insist on holding onto it as evidence. How long that might be will depend on if and when they determine it isn't relevant to any potential prosecution. What's this property you need to retrieve?"

"It's a watch. A special kind of watch that looks like mine." He should remember that well enough.

"If this man is another Travelers' Trust recipient, that will help. Since I represent the trust I can make official inquiries."

Anya shook her head. "He's not, and the watch isn't as special as mine. It can't generate the access codes for the bank." Or do other *special* things. "I can't leave it in the wrong hands though."

The lawyer leaned back in his chair. "If the man is dead, surely that's not a problem anymore. Or do you think the authorities are the wrong hands?"

"I don't know. They might give it to anyone, so I need to make sure it gets into the right hands."

"Alright. If and when the police determine that this watch isn't relevant to their investigation of this

I Have to Do Something

man's death, it could be claimed by his next of kin. I don't suppose that's you?"

If Mr. Hollingsworth meant that she might represent herself inaccurately as this man's family, he'd be disappointed. "I don't even know who he is. Not even his name."

The lawyer looked at her without blinking for a few long moments. "That will make it difficult. But I suppose I can make some inquiries to discover his identity and locate his family and see what might be arranged with them."

Anya took a deep breath and let it out slowly. "I have the resources to pay whatever they ask for, as I am sure you're aware. But since it doesn't belong to him, there shouldn't be any question of sentimental attachment." She looked her lawyer straight in the eye. "I'll pay what *anyone* wants, and since it's not his property, I won't feel any qualms. Whatever you have to do to get it back for me."

He grinned. "I do like to have a free hand, Miss Walker. But I won't do anything illegal. You understand?"

"I wouldn't want you to break the law, Mr. Hollingsworth. But I know you know your way around the law, and if there's a way, you'll find it."

"How can I possibly disappoint such confidence in my abilities? I'll do my best. Now let's see what I can do about your other problem."

Chapter 12

Anya blinked. "What other problem?"

"You said you were down in the lobby with this man's body. There are surveillance cameras covering the whole floor, so the police will at least want to talk to you. Can you tell them anything about how he died?" He gave her a meaningful look.

Anya marked the precise words he had used. "I can't tell them that, no." Now she needed to choose her own words carefully. "I wasn't anywhere nearby when he died. By the time I'd gotten off the elevator into the lobby, the security guards had cordoned off the body and sealed the exits."

Hollingsworth nodded. "The surveillance video is time-stamped, so they will be able to see that for themselves. But they'll be looking through the video to follow every movement the dead man made, from the minute he first entered the building. They'll try to track his movements before that even. Will they see you having any interaction with him?"

Anya found herself blushing as she recalled how she'd run through the lobby with that man chasing her, but that was three years in the past—she didn't think anyone would still remember that. "No, they won't. But I'm afraid they won't see the man entering the building at all." Or Anya herself coming in, not unless they kept the video for three years, which she doubted, and went to the trouble of looking that far back.

Thinking about the investigation from that perspective made Anya wonder what they would see on that video. *Will they see him appear out of thin air? And then fly upward for no apparent reason?* Anya shook her head. "I think the authorities are going to have a real mystery on their hands, figuring out how he died and where he came from."

Mr. Hollingsworth opened his mouth, and Anya could tell he wanted to ask her what she knew about it, and how the man had died. But he thought better of it, and shook his head instead. "If that's the case, they'll likely end up contacting everyone who might have any information—including you. I'm sure they will be collecting the names and addresses of everyone who was in the building around the time of this man's death. Are you going back to your place up in Chickadee?"

"No, I'll be staying at my rooms at the Ngaio until you can get the watch."

"Good. Because if and when they get around to questioning you, or asking you to make any kind of statement, I want to be there. Do you understand?"

Anya smiled. "Of course. But since I have nothing to say, that shouldn't be a problem. My problem is that watch. And I do hope you can find a way to get it."

He fingered his mustache again, trying to hide a grin. "Since the police were never able to keep their

Chapter 12

hands on either of your watches in that other investigation, I can't see how they'd connect you up with this dead man's watch."

Anya shook her head. "No, it seems impossible that they should. But I want that watch before they start taking a close look at it." And start getting any ideas.

"Regardless, I'm going to keep close tabs on this investigation." He stood with a sigh. "You do make my life interesting." He walked around his desk and gestured for her to precede him out of his office. "I think I'd better walk you out of the building. I don't imagine there will be any difficulties, but if I'm with you I know there won't be."

All well and good, Anya thought. But although he'd do his best to get ahold of that watch for her, it might not be enough. She'd leave her lawyer to keep her out of trouble with the authorities, while she did what she could to retrieve that watch, or try to, herself. At least she no longer had to worry about that very dangerous-looking man and what he might do with the watch. But Anya had a responsibility to get it back. There had to be something she could do.

Chapter 13
Anticipating Events

September 16th, 2012 Burnt Ash, Virginia

VERITY drove her Mercedes into the country club parking lot, turning into one of the vacant spots because secretaries didn't avail themselves of the valet service. Generally they did not come here to pester their employers either, but she needed a way to see Hollingsworth away from his home-office, and that meant playing the part of the man's executive secretary. At least she only had to be herself for this role —if any real acting were required, she'd be in trouble.

Stepping out of the car, she smoothed her dress and realized how much she appreciated being back in a conservative skirt suit—what had basically been

Chapter 13

her work uniform for several years. It had only been a few weeks that she'd gone without proper attire—but between quitting her job, marrying Turner, and then chauffeuring Karat around, it felt like forever. The quality wasn't what she was used to, but after a week with Karat, she was running low on funds.

Taking a pregnant woman down to Virginia had slowed her down and tapped her out. Though carting Karat to Hollingsworth, to hand her problems to him—that had been the whole point of the trip. So Verity couldn't very well complain.

She'd discovered where Hollingsworth had disappeared to without much difficulty. It had merely meant returning to her old workplace to face her old boss—Mr. Hemmings was still the branch manager and as disapproving of secretaries who would abandon their posts for marriage as he'd been when she had quit. He'd quite relished being unable to share with her any information he had about recent activities on the part of Travelers' Trust recipients. She didn't work there anymore, and it was confidential. Fortunately he hadn't been able to think of a reason why he couldn't tell her about Hollingsworth.

The lawyer *had* retired his Manhattan practice, then moved back to his Virginia hometown. But the man had been unable to give up the law completely. Now he was a one-man operation working out of his home, with only his wife for a secretary.

Hopefully the club personnel didn't know that—or would assume he'd hired Verity recently. If they challenged her, she'd prepared for that as far as she could, but if she had to appeal to Hollingsworth, she just hoped he would remember her name. After all, for him it had been ten years since he had attended her wedding.

The lawyer supposedly only took cases anymore if they interested him, but Verity believed Karat and her predicament would hook him once he heard. It might be enough to mention the woman's husband's name, if he and Hollingsworth had been old friends as Karat thought. But Verity had to get a chance to talk to the man first.

She herself remained skeptical—not so much of Karat's belief that the lawyer would help her out for the sake of her husband, as this idea that somebody was spying on the woman. Still, Verity had taken a circuitous route from New York City to Burnt Ash—they'd also stayed at cheap motels where they could pay cash and use fake names. It was best to be safe. For that same reason she'd scotched the idea of approaching Hollingsworth at his home. She couldn't risk leading any danger to the man's door. She also didn't want to take the chance that she wouldn't get past that door to make her case.

Upon arriving in Burnt Ash, she had visited the library and gone through back editions of the paper,

Chapter 13

which was how she'd found out Hollingsworth regularly spent time at this club. And she'd decided this would be her best chance to talk to the man without attracting undue attention.

Striding across the blacktop and marching up to the clubhouse entrance, Verity held her slim leather folder confidently in the crook of her arm. The portfolio had cost a pretty penny, but if this didn't work she and Karat would soon be eating at a soup kitchen. And it was an important part of the role she was playing. Verity might not know how to play-act, but she did know how to be a convincing secretary.

Still, she expected to be challenged by the doorman, and she was. "Excuse me, miss, but I don't believe you're a member."

Keeping her face blank, Verity gestured slightly with her leather folder. "No, I'm not. I'm Mr. Hollingsworth's confidential secretary."

The man looked her up and down. "I'm sure he doesn't want to be disturbed. Not here."

She refrained from smiling. "No, I'm quite sure he doesn't. But I require his signature on some documents. And it's urgent—otherwise I wouldn't disturb him for the world."

He nodded at her, but he wasn't happy about it. "Mr. Hollingsworth is in the dining room on the second floor." He opened the door, then ignored her as she glided through.

Verity ascended the stairs and found the dining room easily enough. Thankfully it was mostly empty. Hollingsworth was eating alone at a table by the window, absorbed in finishing off a slice of pie, and she took her time crossing the room to make sure he had plenty of opportunity to notice her.

Reaching his table, she unfastened her portfolio and flipped a couple of sheets over to expose the explanation of Karat and her situation she'd typed up for him. "I'm sorry to interrupt your lunch, sir. But you said you wanted to approve these contracts the minute I had them ready."

Hollingsworth spared a shrewd look for her before focusing on the summary. He skimmed it, then nodded at her. "I see." He reached out and flipped the cover pages back over and, taking a pen she held out for him, scratched an illegible scrawl across the bottom of the page.

Although the summary had included the suspicion of Karat's that someone might be watching her, he didn't as much as glance around. He just continued to act completely normal, as he had when she'd first approached him. She was impressed.

He gave her a brief smile. "And what would you have done if someone had insisted on seeing the papers you were bringing me?"

"Sir! I'm your confidential secretary. I'd guard those papers with my life."

Chapter 13

He grinned wide. "And I'd expect no less." The lawyer combed his salt-and-pepper moustache with his finger. "Now, it'll take me another ten minutes or so to finish my dessert. I'm sure you understand why I'm not inviting you to join me."

Verity nodded. Ten minutes to finish his meal, then the time it would take for the valet to bring his car around. He wanted her to wait for him. She had given him the motel and room number where Karat and she were staying, because he certainly wouldn't want to be seen leaving with her. And he wasn't asking her to follow him, so she presumed he wanted to follow her—to watch for a potential tail?

"Of course, sir. I'll be on my way, then. After I go powder my nose."

No one was close enough to be listening, so they were probably both being far too careful, but it was better that way in her opinion. He seemed to think so too, so she wouldn't worry about his being insufficiently circumspect.

Turning on her heel, Verity marched out of the dining room with a casual glance at her watch—and without looking at anybody else. She continued, out of the clubhouse and across the parking lot. She slid into her Mercedes with a sigh, starting the engine so she could turn the air-conditioning on full-blast and wait for Hollingsworth. Now that it was all over her heart had started racing.

She used the occasion of looking in the rearview mirror and adjusting her makeup to watch for Hollingsworth. When she saw him leaving the club and a valet easing the man's car up to the curb in front of him, Verity pulled out of the parking space and maneuvered the car slowly toward the exit.

After timing it so she left the lot just before Hollingsworth, she forced herself to not look back to see if he was still behind her. She focused on getting to the motel instead. If he lost her, it would not be her fault—he had glanced through the summary so fast, she only hoped he'd recall where to go if he lost her. Ten minutes later she parked outside their room.

She knocked to warn Karat before she unlocked the door, then slipped inside. The ancient air-conditioner was struggling noisily against the heat, and the pregnant woman was propped up, half lying and half sitting on one of the poor excuses for a bed. It was still a relief to be back.

Unfortunately Hollingsworth should show soon enough that Verity wouldn't have an opportunity to rest just yet. Perhaps she was getting old—this past week with Karat had worn her out and left her wearier than she could ever recall being before. She was so tired the knock at the door startled her. Turning to look out the peephole first, she verified it was the lawyer, then let the chain off and flipped the deadbolt, stepping back as she opened the door.

Chapter 13

Hollingsworth strode in and closed the door behind him swiftly. He glanced around the room and ended with a gaze at the ring on Verity's finger.

"An admirable performance, Mrs. Belue. I hope you're still married to the same man?"

She glared at him. "As far as I'm aware." While it had been just over ten years from Hollingsworth's perspective, for Verity it had only been nine days—eight since she'd actually seen her husband.

She saw something in his eyes, and then he was turning to Karat with a little bow. "Mrs. Silverman? Mrs. Miles Silverman?" At her nod, he introduced himself. "I'm Crispin Hollingsworth."

Karat nodded again, her eyes wide. "You were a friend of my husband's."

She'd said that with a hint of a question, and he answered. "Miles and I were good friends together in law school, and I'm sorry to hear about his passing. We may not have kept in touch, but we didn't need to, and I'm obliged to do what I can to help you out. If there's anything I can do."

Karat smiled as her eyes welled with tears. "I'm so glad to finally meet you, Mr. Hollingsworth, but I wish it wasn't this way, coming to you for help. But Miles told me that if I was ever in real trouble, without him around to help—that I should see you."

The lawyer nodded. "Of course. But Mrs. Belue didn't give me many details about your problem."

"Because I haven't told her much about it. And it may take a while—won't you have a seat?"

He looked unsure, but Verity snagged the cheap wooden chair against the wall and placed it behind him so he could sit facing Karat. He gave her a wry grin and sat down, turning back to listen to Karat's tale.

"Please understand that Miles didn't usually tell me about his cases. Confidentiality and all that. It was just this one that worried him so—he was afraid for his client. A government whistleblower. And he wanted me to know the details. He wouldn't tell me the man's name—my husband was very careful not to—in order to protect his identity."

Hollingsworth said nothing, simply gave her his full attention and kept listening.

"One of the senators for our state, of Massachusetts that is, had been using his political influence to harass his mistress. At least, that's what this whistleblower claimed. Miles had been looking into the situation for a few weeks when he was killed."

Karat stopped there, and the tears threatened to start flowing. Hollingsworth nodded and spoke in a gentle voice. "Yes, Mrs. Belue gave me the details of his death, as you told them to her, and why you believe he was murdered. I'll look into that. What I'd like to hear from you now are any details you know about this harassment."

Chapter 13

She sniffed and nodded and continued. "This is all second-hand, you understand? What Miles told me his client had told him. He said Senator Souseman had been having an affair with some waitress and gotten her pregnant. And that when she'd demanded support and threatened to go to the press if he didn't come through—"

"Yes?"

"Well, apparently this woman already had a kid, a daughter in elementary school, and the next thing she knew the Department of Education had showed up at her apartment with a SWAT team and a search warrant. Supposedly they found some unapproved math textbooks and threatened to take her daughter away from her. He said the senator sent her a message—to stop making trouble or else she would lose her daughter *and* be audited by the IRS."

The lawyer sighed. "Thankfully those abuses of power are rare, but they do happen, and they should never be tolerated. But without the whistleblower, I don't know what I can do. You don't have his name, but do you know how I can get in contact with him?"

Karat shook her head. "I don't know anything—the man was scared, and Miles was so afraid for him that he didn't want there to be any more contact between them than necessary. He said it was up to his client to get in touch, and only when and how he felt safe. Does this mean you can't help?"

Hollingsworth smiled. "It means I may not be able to do anything about the senator, though we'll see. I think I can at least do something to help with your situation. The most important thing is to make sure you, and your baby, are safe—that means moving you to a safer location while I see about setting you up with a new identity."

"A new identity?"

"It's the only way I won't worry about you while I try to find a more permanent way to protect you. I think you know far too much for Senator Souseman to be comfortable, if he's aware of it. Let's hope he's not."

Verity was thinking she wouldn't put money on that chance. Karat's flight from home and falling off the radar should be enough to convince the senator, if he needed convincing, that she could be a threat to him. Then Verity became aware that the lawyer was pulling his wallet from inside his jacket and looking at her. He withdrew a sheaf of hundred dollar bills, and after a brief hesitation he also removed a credit card, then handed it all to her.

"That Mercedes, parked outside a place like this for too long—it will attract attention, and any attention paid to you at this point would be bad. Besides, you girls shouldn't have to stay at a dump like this." He nodded at what he'd given her. "Use the cash to get whatever food or clothes you'll need and use the

Chapter 13

card to check into the Granger hotel—that should be classy enough to go with your brand new Mercedes. The card is for business expenses, and I'll see you're authorized on the account. Just make sure you keep the receipts, and you can itemize everything back at the office."

Verity was nonplussed. "Back at the office?"

"Consider this your lunch break. After you settle Mrs. Silverman at the hotel, you can get to work helping me set her up with a new identity. You are my confidential secretary, aren't you?"

"Yes, sir." That solved her own problem of how she would get along while waiting for Turner or one of the others to find her. It was likely enough one of them would be running to Hollingsworth for help at some point. But if not—if none of the Travelers had shown up come summer, she'd be checking again at the house in Chickadee.

Until then, she could help the lawyer help Karat, who had problems much bigger than Verity's.

Chapter 14

The Good Samaritans

September 11th, 1962 The Chihuahuan Desert

TURNER forced himself to walk slow. He was on the downward slope of a foothill on the other side of the mountains, and if he wasn't careful he'd tumble to the bottom head first. Those small, spiny agave plants that had been trying to shred his pants legs to rags still threatened his shins, but he had a lot more respect for them now—if only he'd known that those sharp stalks contained beautiful, wonderful water.

The water that MacInnes had provided had revived Turner just in time. He hadn't been sweating too much, even in the daytime, when the air was hot enough to bake him, but he still needed to replenish the water he lost, or he wouldn't last very long. Now

Chapter 14

he could at least stay hydrated with the help of those nasty little plants.

MacInnes had also recommended some paddle-shaped cactus as food. But Turner would have to be desperately hungry before he ate anything like that, and he knew he could survive for days without solid food. If he had to.

The ground began leveling off, but he continued carefully—while there was most of a moon, giving a little light to see where he put his feet, a wrong step could be disastrous. He certainly couldn't see much in the distance—but supposedly the road was there, somewhere, and he wasn't likely to miss it. At least he'd gotten this far before dawn. He hoped he could reach the highway while it remained dark and cool. *You could even send me a ride before the sun comes out to cook me again.*

MacInnes had said there wasn't much traffic, so Turner didn't know how long he might have to wait for someone to come along, much less someone who was willing to give him a lift to civilization—though he was beginning to doubt such a thing really existed—and as long as he loitered by the road, he would have no shelter from the sun.

As he kept walking, he wondered where his wife was, what Verity was doing. And with a shock he realized how little he'd been thinking of her in the past couple of days. He knew she could take care of herself, and he'd rather a lot to deal with himself. But still.

Walking steadily south, he caught himself worrying, and firmly resisted those anxieties—he loved Verity, he had married her, and he missed her. But unless something extraordinary happened—and extraordinary things did happen, Turner thought with a grin—it would be a long time before he saw Verity again. What good would it do him to mope around and let himself get depressed by dwelling on something he couldn't do anything about?

If by some miracle he and his wife were soon reunited, all well and good. But the only thing Turner could do for Verity now was survive—and pray. *I've turned her over into Your hands, Lord, and I'll keep doing that until I can leave her there.*

The first dim reflection of light across the land, from a sun still hiding behind those higher peaks to the east, cast enough illumination for Turner to see the road ahead of him in the distance—two hundred meters or so away. Too far yet, when he saw a semi roaring down the highway, to try hitching a ride.

But sighting his goal was enough to lift Turner's spirit and lighten his steps, and start him considering what he would do if and when he reached civilization. His ID was no good. He didn't know about his cash, but there was enough light to check now so he pulled out his wallet and fanned through the bills

Chapter 14

peering at the years they were printed—and realized that none of them would be worth anything.

Turner stopped in his tracks and sighed. His ID and cash from the future would all be taken as counterfeit, and the bank account Page had set up for his use wouldn't exist for decades. His billfold was the only thing of any use—everything in it would actually be a liability. He wouldn't want them to be found in his possession. And all of it could be replaced, if and when he made it back to the future.

So while it was still dim and the road far off, he found a natural deep depression in the sand, of the kind he'd been trying to avoid stumbling into—then dumped it all at the bottom, his identification, cash, and bank card. He took a few minutes to kick a load of dirt on top of it all and carefully stomp down and pack it tight. He'd just buried Turner Belue, possibly forever.

He started again toward the highway, considering that if he were to remain so far back in the past for any length of time, he should work to establish a new identity for himself—one that wouldn't get confused with his twenty-first century self. Turner was his real name, and he wouldn't give that up. Belue, though, he had chosen specifically to give to Verity. If only someone, probably Page, had not added the extra 'e' it would've been perfect for her. He'd have to come up with a new last name for his new life.

He reached the side of the road and saw that so much dust had blown over it he might not have seen it in the dark. Looking down the dusty pavement to the west and the east, he had two choices—since he didn't want to just stand there waiting, not when he could be walking in one direction or another and at least getting closer to civilization. Even if from what MacInnes had said, it was too far in either direction to think he could actually make it. Though it would put the sun in his eyes, he felt sure east was the way he should go. He'd just have to shade his eyes with his hand.

Once the sun had fully risen over the tall peaks ahead, Turner found himself laughing out loud, and it was a harsh sound in the quiet, empty desert. He wondered if he was becoming hysterical. The entire experience of what he was going through might be making him mad.

Twice someone sped past him. The first time it was a sedan he didn't hear until it was almost upon him. Either they didn't see him waving or ignored it and drove on without slowing. The second time he heard the engine of the pickup before he saw it, and waved mightily with both arms as it approached. It was coming toward him from the east and slowed at least. Blinded by the sun in his eyes, he couldn't see the driver of the truck, but that driver must've seen him. And apparently hadn't liked what he saw.

Chapter 14

Eventually it became too much for Turner, with the full force of the sun coming directly at him. And he was weary from walking and sweating heavily. So when he saw the boulder by the side of the road, just off the shoulder and just big enough to sit on—but not big enough to provide any shade—he decided to stop.

At least he could rest while he roasted. So, turning his back to the sun and facing west, he sat down on the rock and closed his eyes and waited. *I don't know what I'm waiting for, but You do.*

He had a lot yet to learn, and he needed wisdom to find his way, so he sat there and listened. There, away from the slightest hint of civilization, he found a peace deeper than he'd ever known, and he heard what was in his heart.

How long he had sat there, listening, before he heard something else, he didn't know. But when he finally noticed the sound of the engine, it was idling —and he hadn't moved a muscle. Then the noise of the engine stopped and there was a brief moment of silence before two doors were slammed.

Then came a woman's voice, close at hand. "Is it some kind of sculpture do you think? Bob?"

A man's voice, presumably Bob's, answered. "I think it's a man. Perhaps some kind of performance art?"

"Out here in the middle of nowhere?"

Turner could hear Bob shaking his head. "Why would it make any more sense for a sculpture to be 'out here in the middle of nowhere'?"

"A person would have to be crazy. Sitting there like a statue in this heat would kill them quick."

"Maybe it's a corpse. But if so, it's a remarkably well-preserved corpse."

The woman snorted. "Well this *is* the desert."

Slowly and carefully opening his dry and creaky eyelids, Turner saw the couple standing only a little distance in front of him, watching him. Behind the pair a dust-coated jeep was parked on the shoulder. These two were dressed for the desert, in sleeveless t-shirts and khaki shorts and broad-brimmed hats. They looked like they were on safari.

The woman gasped and pointed. "You're right, Bob. It is a man, and I think he's alive."

Turner tried to clear his throat before speaking, but his words came out as a croak. "I don't believe dead men can talk. As far as I'm aware, anyway."

Startled, the pair both jumped backward. Then the man took a cautious step forward and spoke. "I hope you can tell me what you're doing out here."

"Actually, I was hoping somebody would come along and offer me a ride."

The man and woman looked at each other, then back to Turner. "Where to?"

"I'm not picky. Anywhere there's shelter."

Chapter 14

The woman smiled back. "Well, we're not going to leave you here to die. I don't think it's your time yet."

Turner nodded. "Apparently not."

Bob took another step forward, offering a hand which Turner took and shook, and held on to while he slowly stood.

"I'm Bob, by the way, and this is my wife, Joy."

"Turner, and I'm pleased." And that was an understatement.

"You can ride in the back of our jeep, if that's alright. Do you need help getting in?"

Turner managed a grin. "Thanks, but I think I can make it."

Still, Bob gave him a hand before climbing into the driver's seat. Joy twisted around in the passenger seat to stare at Turner with undisguised curiosity. "You're wearing a wedding ring. Where's your wife? Will she be worried?" She turned to Bob. "I think we should stop at the nearest phone so he can call and let her know he's okay."

Clearing his throat, Turner interjected before it could go any further. "I don't know—where my wife is or how I could get in contact. I can only hope she isn't worried about me."

Joy shook her head. "If she could see you now, I'm sure she'd be worried. Your nice clothes are all caked with dust—I don't think they can be saved."

An involuntary groan escaped Turner's lips. It wouldn't help to worry about his clothes though. He needed to think about what kind of job he could get with no identification. It would likely be something menial, so nice clothes wouldn't be necessary.

Joy kept staring at him. "We're the McMillans, since Bob didn't say. And you're Turner—"

He hesitated a moment. Now was the time he'd have to pick a new name for himself. Turner Learner? That would make his hypothetical parents seem like idiots. "Hope. I'm Turner Hope." Because that was what he'd found, and that was what he needed.

Joy barked a laugh. "Any relation to Bob?"

That confused him. "Didn't you just say he was a McMillan? How would we be related?"

Bob glanced over at his wife. "See, he's a comedian. One of those deadpan types. Didn't I tell you he was a performer?"

"You said a 'performance artist', dear. Which is different. I think Turner just has a refined sense of humor. Unlike you, dear."

That comment only made Bob guffaw loudly. It was an easy banter between them which Turner envied—he and Verity might never have the opportunity to develop that kind of comfortable intimacy. He very well might never see her again.

He had looked forward to seeing what their life together would be like. But he might never find out.

Chapter 14

Thinking like that, though, would definitely depress him if he kept at it. He had to trust that there was a purpose to everything he was going through, and he felt confident he'd find out what that was. Eventually. *What I know for sure is that You haven't finished with me yet.*

Chapter 15

Out of the Frying Pan

October 23rd, 1918 Midtown Manhattan

MATT found himself sitting on the ground right in the middle of Thirty-fourth Street. He rolled out of the way of an oncoming car and jogged to the sidewalk, thankful that the traffic was much lighter than it had been just a moment ago. Looking down at his watch, his heart leapt to see he had Traveled exactly three years into the future. He wanted to pump his fist in the air in celebration, but his hands were still cuffed together.

He glanced around without thinking, searching for Page, but of course she wasn't there—they'd taken him a few blocks away from where she had been when she'd Traveled, before he could follow.

Chapter 15

At least Matt had arrived on the day he'd aimed at. All those hours pouring over and struggling with the watch's programming had paid off when tested. He'd discovered that the time-travel app on the professor's device contained, for some reason, a limited Traveling program as a subroutine—what appeared to be the same app as on Page's watch, the one that enabled her to Travel up to three years but could not change her physical location. *Not intentionally.*

So Matt had hoped he could accurately Travel a shorter temporal distance, but he'd balked at trying out this theory—until he'd been forced to by circumstance. And it had worked just as he'd supposed. It had caught him up with Page after she had jumped three years into the future, inadvertently abandoning him. He wanted to start tracking her down right away.

First though, he'd have to get out of these handcuffs. Already he was garnering some strange looks from a few pedestrians gliding along. He raised his manacled hands and waved at a man nearby before turning and strolling in the opposite direction. If he acted natural, hopefully he could get where he needed without being molested.

Whistling while he walked, Matt casually raised his wrist and flipped to the locator screen to see the blip or bar that would give him an idea where Page was now. But once again there was nothing. Biting back a curse, he changed over to the temporal tuner to see she was right here, in Midtown Manhattan on the same date, in the same hour. It was when he returned to the regular watch face and saw what time it was, in his own personal time, that he realized he had landed nine minutes ahead of Page. *Better than two weeks ahead.* And much better than three years behind her.

Being unable to use the locator app for tracking her, though, put Matt right back where he had been three years ago—searching for Page among the vast throngs crowding Manhattan. Not that they were in evidence at the moment. Actually, his situation had improved—since today was a Wednesday, the banks should be open. Page would likely head to the main branch of their bank soon, so that should be his first stop too. After he'd gotten himself freed from these handcuffs.

When Matt saw the squat brick precinct house of Midtown South, he was grateful it had stayed where it was for over eighty years into the future so he was able to find it so easily now—even if it had inexplicably changed its precinct number. Holding his hands in the air in front of him, Matt waved to the cops he met as he approached the entrance. Since they saw he was not trying to hide what he was doing, nobody tried to stop him. He bounded up the steps and into the lobby, straight to the sergeant at the duty desk.

Chapter 15

Matt lifted his hands to make sure the man saw his predicament. "Good day, sergeant. Can you get these things off me?"

The man gaped for a moment before recovering his poise. Peering closely at the handcuffs Matt was waving in front of his face, he shook his head sadly. "We haven't used that kind for a couple of years or so. What have you been playing at, son? You trying to be another Harry Houdini?"

Matt grinned. "Actually, yes. I thought I did alright, but now I'm stuck in these things."

The sergeant sighed and came around the desk. "I'll just sit you down someplace while I check to see you haven't escaped from somewhere."

"Like a looney bin?"

"Then we'll see about getting those things off of you." The man escorted him down a corridor, muttering something about 'students' and 'pranks'.

Matt meekly followed the sergeant to a drab little room that looked like the kind of place the police used to interview suspects on television. Hopefully, an interrogation wasn't imminent. Allowing the police to assume he was a student was one thing, but if they questioned him, he certainly couldn't tell them the truth. And no story would stand up to scrutiny. But unless someone from three years ago had a really good memory, the sergeant should find that Matt hadn't escaped from custody and let him loose.

The sergeant sat Matt down in a rickety wooden chair. "You just wait here comfortably while I make some calls. I dare say somebody might bring you a cup of coffee if it takes too long." He left the room, closing the door behind him but not locking it. *Unnecessary inside a police station?*

The threatened cup of coffee, which would surely have been as bad as anything out of one of those vending machines in the future, never materialized. But twenty minutes later a plain-clothes policeman did enter the tiny room.

"My name is Lieutenant Cross. Mr.—"

"Walker. Matt Walker."

"The sergeant said you looked like a college student. One who's been in a bit of a tussle?"

"I'm a graduate student." He *was* still a student eighty-four years in the future. Matt rubbed his jaw where he'd been socked three years ago. "And I objected to a remark someone made about a girl I fancy, and he popped me one."

Lt. Cross nodded. "Knocked you to the ground, looks like."

Matt grinned. "I must look a picture. I need to change clothes, but that's a little difficult wearing a pair of handcuffs."

"You must've been wearing them when you got slugged." He sighed. "I don't suppose you're pressing charges against whoever hit you?"

Chapter 15

Matt shook his head while the lieutenant took a ring of keys from his pocket and unlocked the cuffs. "I'd like to give you a lecture, or several, but I know my words would fall on deaf ears." He removed the manacles and stuffed them in his pocket along with the keys. "I'll just hold on to them, so whatever mischief you get into, it'll have to be without handcuffs the next time."

Matt let his grin disappear and nodded solemnly before slipping out the open door. The man could always change his mind about that lecture, and Matt didn't need it. It wasn't as if New York City in nineteen eighteen was overflowing with violent crime. *It will come soon enough, though.*

Massaging his chafed wrists and giving the sergeant at the desk a manacle-free wave, Matt left the precinct house and took a big lungful of sweet fresh air. *Free at last.* Now he had to hurry to find Page. He let his long legs carry him effortlessly down one block after another, aware of the time he'd lost and already knowing where to head next. The bank.

If Page hadn't shown up yet at the main branch of the American International State Bank to get her money, she would soon. After that would probably come shopping—which reminded Matt he needed a new outfit, and all his baggage had been sent to the hotel he'd made a reservation for three years ago. *I wonder what they did with my stuff.*

Out of the Frying Pan

When he reached the right corner, he found the bank looking pretty much the same as it ever would and began to dread facing another Mr. Pitt or even a Mr. Hemmings. He didn't know why they shouldn't give him a good reception, though. He'd kept most of the money he'd taken from the trust stipend, both in nineteen twelve and three years later, sitting in a savings account. And before he'd set out on his trip three years ago, he'd had them transfer his account here to the main branch. He was a little late, but he should still be a valued customer.

So Matt breezed into the lobby trying to smile—and his eyes searched the place for Page. She'd had enough time to get here, but he didn't see her. Maybe she was already with the manager somewhere in the back, getting another chunk of money out of the trust.

Like everywhere he'd seen since arriving in this time, the bank was mostly empty. Matt wondered if something important was going on somewhere, but he was glad it meant he could walk right up to a teller's window without waiting in line. "I need to see the branch manager. Could you let him know Matt Walker is here about the Travelers' Trust?" If Page was with the man when the message was delivered, that would be that.

The young man nodded, then closed his window and darted away. A minute later, a stout man wear-

Chapter 15

ing a dark three-piece suit barreled out of a back office. He took a look at Matt's nice, but rather rumpled togs and smiled.

"Mr. Walker, we expected to see you three years ago. We're glad you made it alright. I'm Douglass, by the way."

He wasn't the stereotypical banker Matt had expected. Was he using the royal 'we' or was the man speaking corporately for the bank? "Well, *I'm* glad I finally made it. Traveling a great distance poses its difficulties, you know. I don't suppose a pretty redhead has already shown up today? It couldn't have been very long ago."

"Are you saying Miss Page is back in town? We haven't seen her since—" Mr. Douglass looked into the ceiling. "About three years ago, as it happens."

Enough time had passed for Page to have come here already, if this was going to be her first stop, or to have gone just about anywhere in the city. "Then I expect her to stop by soon. But I don't know where she's staying, so I'd appreciate it if you'd give her a message from me when she comes."

The banker nodded readily. "Of course, certainly. No trouble at all. But don't you have business of your own you need to attend to?"

Matt nodded. While he wanted to be out there, searching for Page, visiting stores all over Midtown would be a long and likely fruitless task. "I might as well withdraw some of my money—I think I'll need plenty. Thank you, Mr. Douglass. But I'll wait before requesting funds from this year's stipend, until I have a better idea how long I'll be sticking around." Which would depend on Page.

Mr. Douglass laughed heartily. "Of course, certainly. Glad to be of service." He looked at the teller. "Tyler, help this man take out some of his money. Don't let him take it all, though." He turned to Matt again, still laughing. "Isn't that right, sir? You have to leave us something."

Matt almost believed he preferred Mr. Pitt and his dry disapproval. Evidently not every banker was made from the same mold. "About this message for Miss Page. Please tell her I'll be staying at the Hotel Ngaio across the street. I'm hoping they have a vacancy. If not, I'll come back and let you know where I end up getting a room. Alright?"

The man had stopped laughing and looked a bit startled. "The Ngaio? Of course they'll have a room for you. Who doesn't have plenty of vacancies these days?"

Matt remembered the year and supposed it was a side effect of the war, that even New York City had been thinned out. "Then please tell her that's where she can find me. And now your clerk can get me my money, and you can get back to your business. I'm sure you're a busy man."

Chapter 15

"You can say that again. But if you do need any more help, I'll be available."

"I'll remember that." As soon as the banker had bustled away, Matt turned to Tyler to fill out a withdrawal slip.

Once he'd refilled the contents of his wallet, he walked out of the bank and across the street and into the lobby of the Ngaio. Striding up to the clerk at the desk, Matt took one of his new twenties and slid it across the counter. "I need a room." Remembering the banker's comments about vacancies, he took a chance and continued. "And if room 412 is available, that would be great. Also, I had my luggage delivered here—"

"Yes, sir. The name?"

Matt grinned. "Matt Walker. But I had it sent three years ago, so you may have a hard time finding it."

The clerk goggled for a moment before recovering. "Indeed, sir. It may take us a while. And room 412 *is* available. You know that's one of our luxury suites?"

"I've stayed there—" He was about to say in the past, but it had been the future. "Previously. It has a sentimental attachment." He took another twenty and handed it to the clerk. "When you find my bags, and I hope you'll make every effort, just have them put in my room." *If* they were found.

The man nodded. "If you'll please sign the register." The clerk slid the book toward Matt and then grabbed a key from behind the counter and handed it over.

Since he didn't have any baggage to leave in his room, Matt simply turned and stalked out of the hotel to begin looking for Page. For the next few hours he went from one upscale shop to another, describing Page to various clerks and saleswomen without success. Most of them wanted to be helpful, but he couldn't find anyone who'd actually seen her. With so many stores in Midtown alone, it was worse odds than playing the lottery, but he kept at it.

At one upscale department store, he did have a different kind of success. He stopped in at the men's department and took time to buy himself a few new outfits, lightweight suits of the latest cut. Of course he had to stand around while they took his measurements, but he insisted on wearing one of them out of the store, even if it hadn't been tailored to him yet. The rest of his suits and the other clothes he had ordered would be delivered to his hotel room the next day, but at least he had clean clothes to wear in the interim. And he wouldn't have to worry whether or not the Ngaio found his luggage.

He went on and made further enquiries at more shops, and found the saleswoman more eager to be of help now, but he didn't find any trace of Page. It

Chapter 15

was an extremely long day. Matt was weary, worn, and hungry at the end of it—too tired to sit down for a formal meal somewhere. He stopped at a cart selling meat-filled buns and bought a couple—without asking what the meat might be, he was just grateful for the fuel. He consumed his dinner as he walked back to the hotel. He had done all he could for one day.

By the time he was striding back into the lobby, it had grown dark out, and while the city was bright enough, it wasn't anything like it would be one day. He was glad to walk into the well-lit hotel, and even gladder that he already had his room key. He was so exhausted he even took the elevator up to the fourth floor, and he trudged down the hall to his room with his strength flagging.

He needed plenty of rest. So opening the door, he took the 'please do not disturb' placard and hung it on the outside. That sign ought to keep the maids from disturbing him if he slept late, but it would not stop Page if she dropped by the bank in the morning and discovered he was here. And then he nearly forgot to lock the door behind him.

Falling into the bed barely before he'd managed to take off his shoes, Matt realized he was exhausted —and those meat-filled buns weren't sitting well on his stomach. But he was still young, and even if he'd had a long day, he shouldn't feel so fatigued.

Thinking he must've gotten old fast with all the time-traveling, Matt rolled over onto his back with a groan. He was too tired to pull back the bedspread. He told himself it hardly mattered. What did matter was getting up and getting out of his new suit before it got too rumpled, but he didn't have the energy.

Then he put his hand to his forehead—and felt a searing heat. He had a fever. *For once I pushed myself too hard.*

Then he recalled that nineteen eighteen wasn't just the last year of the First World War—it was also the time of that great influenza pandemic that killed millions. Matt knew it had hit the eastern portion of the country hard in the fall, near the end of the war. And he remembered that it had been the young and healthy who had suffered the most fatalities.

He thought he ought to call the hotel desk clerk and ask for a doctor to be sent up. Or go to a hospital. He had a notion neither of those were good ideas, but he wasn't sure why—he seemed to be having a difficult time thinking clearly. But it didn't matter. He didn't have the strength to get out of bed, much less do anything else.

Chapter 16
Playing with Fire

October 23rd, 1918 Midtown Manhattan

PAGE pressed the elevator call button and listened to the antiquated contraption as it rumbled up from the lobby—while she continued alternating between states of concern and consternation over the events of the day. She might be able to settle on one particular attitude if she knew what had really happened. If Matt was alive and well, she could be mad at him, but if he wasn't—

She wasn't going to let herself think about that, she told herself for the twenty-seventh time. It had all started so well. She had been having a great time with the suffragettes, marching in a parade up Fifth Avenue. Then she'd spied Matt in the crowd watching her. He'd finally found her and everything was wonderful. Then of course, he'd gotten himself into some trouble, and she'd run to his rescue, Traveling him away from the men he was fighting and the police who were closing in on him. Or she thought she had.

When she'd appeared the next moment in nineteen eighteen, she hadn't been able to see Matt anywhere. Which wasn't surprising—he would've come through farther away from her. He hadn't appeared as a blip on her locator screen either, but she wasn't sure that had been working properly. But even if his locator app was malfunctioning too, he should have known exactly where to find her.

Page had stood there, waiting right where she'd left from, on one side of Fifth Avenue, and growing more and more irritated with Matt not showing up. Until she'd finally given up on lingering around.

The elevator came to rest with a thump, and the doors slid open. She watched the elevator boy grab the grill from the other side and drag it back with a horrible clacking noise. Normally she wouldn't take the elevator down from the fourth floor to the lobby, but it had been a long day—so she stepped in and let herself be lowered to the ground floor.

After the boy had repeated the elaborate procedure to allow her to get out, she passed him a quarter and smiled. "Thank you, Willim."

Chapter 16

As she glided out onto the plush carpet, the boy muttered at her back. "It's Bobby, miss."

Page had waited for Matt as long as she could—but she'd had urgent business to take care of. Like clothes. In her haste to Travel Matt out of the trouble he'd gotten himself into, Page had left behind all her luggage, leaving her with only the clothes she'd been wearing. Shopping had become an emergency instead of entertainment—which seemed to be a recurring phenomenon since she'd been with Matt.

Passing through the lobby and on into the dining room, Page glanced around at the mostly deserted place. A man with thick black hair and wearing evening dress leaned back sipping his drink by himself, and a middle-aged couple in their Sunday best leaned forward looking at their menus. Page wondered what fare the Ngaio would be offering in this time of austerity.

The lone waiter guided her to a small table and presented her with a menu and asked if she wanted a preprandial drink. She declined and stared at the selection of appetizers while her mind drifted. She had stayed in San Francisco as a guest in Margaret and Nancy's house for almost three weeks, helping them organize their trip to join the suffrage parade in New York City. She'd enjoyed that, and the train trip across the country. And then the parade itself. It had all been fun up to that one point.

Page remembered the look of alarm she'd seen on Matt's face, probably more worry for her than for his own situation. And though she'd done what she could to help him, she had lost him again. Now she was eating alone.

She'd felt all on her own since arriving in nineteen eighteen—an afternoon of visiting various and sundry shops to find the right clothes, with a break for tea, and all the while waiting, hoping for Matt to just show up again like he had at the parade, but no. She'd finally ended up at the Ngaio in a wave of nostalgia and taken a room, and a nice long nap. Now she was refreshed, but what for? A meal by herself, in the middle of Manhattan.

The streets and the shops had both been mostly deserted, just like the hotel restaurant. That meant she'd had the saleswomen all to herself as she chose some of the new fashions—which were a definite improvement—the hemlines were a bit higher, and the skirts were less layered and less cumbersome, offering more freedom of movement. However, between the war and the flu, people weren't feeling especially gay. Even her new violet dress with matching high heels could not lift her spirits up above the somber mood around her.

Luckily she'd had plenty of cash on her in nineteen fifteen when she'd Traveled. So she'd skipped going to the bank and concentrated on getting these

Chapter 16

new outfits—to go with the dress she wore now, she had picked up a light silk jacket in glossy green with brass buttons. Just the thing to wear out on a nippy night out on the town with Matt. But he wasn't anywhere around. Yet.

When she wasn't being upset with Matt for not being there, she was worrying that he'd managed to get himself into some trouble he hadn't been able to get out of. And without knowing where he was, she couldn't do anything to help him. She would simply have to hope he would be alright—and this time she would stay put and wait for him to find her, again.

Page looked down at her plate and saw that she had finished off her Chicken Kiev without even realizing she'd ordered. Well, she had woken from her nap hungry. Buying new clothes had been tiring instead of fun, and now she'd eaten mechanically and unconsciously rather then enjoying her food.

It was in the middle of this pensive abstraction that a shadow fell across her. Expecting the return of the waiter, Page glanced up and was surprised to see the tall, dark and handsome gentleman who had been dining all by his lonesome on the other side of the room.

His voice was smooth. "A beautiful young woman such as yourself should not be dining alone. It is unusual. But since we have both finished our meals on our own, perhaps you'll permit me to buy drinks, and you can tell me all about yourself. Are you perhaps one of these modern adventuresses one reads about?"

"I don't drink alcohol, if that's what you mean." But Page could use the company. "Maybe we could share an after-dinner coffee though?"

He smiled and slid into the seat beside her, signaling to the waiter as he did so. "And you are?"

"Page. And I suppose you would call me an adventuress."

"And I am Henry Riggleston, the Second. But of course you recognized me?"

"I didn't. Should I have? And wouldn't that be 'Junior' rather than 'the Second'?"

His smile faltered for a moment but recovered. "You are a very bold and independent woman, Miss Page, and I appreciate that very much." The waiter appeared at the table, and Riggleston turned to address him. "Two coffees, please. Make mine Irish." He deftly slipped the man a bill before turning back to her. "You will permit me something stronger, I'm sure. While I still can."

"What do you mean, while you can?"

His smile widened. "Of course it's nice to find a modern woman such as yourself who doesn't know about politics, but I would've thought everyone was aware that they've sent Prohibition to be ratified by the states. And I'm afraid it will be."

Chapter 16

Page looked him up and down. Not only was he suave and impeccably dressed, but the man was the very image of the twentieth century Romeo she had envisioned. "Do you dance?"

Riggleston nodded. "You are not only beautiful but a mind reader. I was going to suggest that after we enjoy our coffee, you accompany me to this fabulous club I know. They have a large ballroom and a very modern big band that plays the tango. Do you tango, Page?"

"I'd like to, but I've never learned how."

"Then I will teach you, and I promise you it will be a very pleasurable experience. I am a very experienced man. A man of the world, you know."

Page was tempted. It all sounded very romantic of course. *And if Matt isn't going to show up to take me dancing, why shouldn't I?* She wouldn't do herself any favors by sitting in her room, brooding.

She opened her mouth to accept the invitation. "Perhaps tomorrow night? I only arrived today and I'm tired." Then if Matt still hadn't appeared by tomorrow night, she could go out on the town and enjoy herself.

"The coffee will revive you, I'm sure, and it's far too early to call it a night. The evening has only begun. But you are right that we should save a public debut until I've taught you the tango, so you will not mind dancing with everyone's eyes on you."

While the waiter came and set their cups of coffee down in front of them, Page considered mastering the tango before meeting Matt again. "The ballroom here at the Ngaio is probably empty."

Riggleston shook his head. "Undoubtedly. Because they have no band except on the weekends. I will take you up to my suite, where there is plenty of space, and show you how to dance."

"I don't know…" She didn't like that idea. Taking a sip of coffee, she almost choked. "I believe the waiter gave me your cup by mistake." They'd added a hefty slug of spirits to make it Irish.

"You don't like it?" He shook his head and took his cup and saucer, placing it in front of her and taking hers in turn. "Since you don't drink, maybe you were just unprepared for the taste."

Page took a sip of her black, unadulterated coffee with a sigh. "That's better."

"If you say so. At least it will help you stay alert—we have a long night ahead of us."

"I told you I'm tired. I really don't think I'm up to dancing lessons tonight. Maybe tomorrow."

"Of course. I will escort you to your room—then you will get the rest you need. For tomorrow will be quite memorable, I assure you." He downed his coffee in a few big swigs.

Page took several more sips hoping to perk up a bit. She was going to need to be on her toes to deal

Chapter 16

with Mr. Riggleston—at least she was learning a lot about twentieth century Romeos.

Setting her cup back on the saucer she smiled a bit. "I think I'll cut the evening short, then. Thanks for the offer of an escort, but I don't need the assistance."

He stood and extended his hand. "Nonsense. I insist, my dear. It would be unchivalrous of me not to see you safely to your bed."

Page definitely didn't like him addressing her in that familiar manner, or talking in that sly manner, but she didn't want to make an issue of it right here and now. But she felt sure he wasn't going to simply say goodbye and leave her at her door.

Feeling a little wobbly on her feet, she rose with as much grace as possible and strode out of the dining room and across the lobby with Riggleston hurrying after her. If she'd been alone, she'd probably have taken the stairs. Instead she went straight for the elevator. That would keep her from being alone with Riggleston—and give her an opportunity.

She nodded to the boy as she stepped in. "Good evening, Bobby." Riggleston had followed her into the car, and she turned to talk to him in a firm tone. "My room is on the third floor, but you really don't need to escort me there. I'm sure this hotel is safe."

"But you must permit me the pleasure of seeing you to your room and giving you a proper adieu."

Shaking her head at this, Page felt a bit woozy. She swayed as the elevator climbed, and stumbled—Riggleston reached out to take her elbow and steadied her.

"I think because you do not drink, that one sip has gone to your head. The proper cure would be to have another drink, and my penthouse suite has an excellent bar."

"No, thank you. I think resting in my room will be all the cure I need."

The elevator shuddered to a halt and Bobby announced, "Third floor, miss," in a loud voice before opening the grill for them.

Page turned back as Riggleston exited the car—she opened her reticule to find a dollar bill to tip the boy. She leaned in and pressed it into his hand and waited until the doors had closed before turning to Riggleston with wide eyes. "I *must* be a little drunk—I forgot to get my room key from the front desk."

She turned back and affected surprise at seeing the elevator was already on its way down. "I'll have to take the stairs." So saying, she was already walking down the corridor several steps and opening the door to the stairwell.

She heard Riggleston crying "Wait!" behind her as she let the door swing shut and slipped her heels off and padded up the stairs with speed and stealth. She heard the door opening below her and clomping

Chapter 16

as Riggleston stamped his way down to the lobby, as she alighted on the fourth floor landing. She steadied herself on the railing and let out a silent sigh. It was too soon to relax her guard, though.

Emerging into the corridor, she scurried to her room, unlocked the door and swooped inside. She turned both locks and slid the chain across. After a moment's thought, she dragged a heavy armchair in from the sitting room and shoved it against the door —she wasn't taking any chances.

With a bit of a warning, she could always Travel away from him of course. But she didn't like to run away, and she ought to be clever enough to not have to. Besides, Traveling would only make it more difficult for Matt to find her—and he was taking a long time as it was.

So running would be a last resort, right after the option of stabbing Riggleston in self-defense. That thought brought a smile to her face. But she would do better to avoid any confrontation at all with him —though that might be difficult.

Certainly Riggleston would learn where to find her—a small tip to the clerk would give the man her room number. She'd just have to outsmart him. An easy enough proposition, she thought. He wouldn't be a morning person, so if she needed to go out, she could go early. She had enough funds to wait a few days before going to the bank, and she could call the store she'd ordered new clothes from and make sure they delivered as early as possible. But those would be only temporary measures while she came up with something better, more permanent.

Surely there was another solution besides stabbing a man. Page could not think clearly right then, but a good night's sleep would help with that, and if she took a while to decide what to do, it didn't matter. She had no reason to rush.

Chapter 17
Nye in the Soup

July 15th, 2003 Midtown Manhattan

NYE kept her eye on 'George'—or at least her glasses did—as she ladled plenty of the delicious cabbage soup into a bowl for the next person in line. George had let some stubble grow and taken to rubbing dirt on his face, but it was too late. He'd already attracted her attention. Even had she not previously identified him, it was not a disguise that would've fooled her facial recognition software. He must have been worried she'd recall his face anyway, and know him for who he was, since he kept turning that face away from her. *But what's he doing here?*

He sat sipping delicately at his cabbage soup at one of the tables near the entrance, and nibbling on his bread in between great gulps of coffee. And Nye reviewed her video of him and looked for clues.

Shortly after she had volunteered to help out at this soup kitchen, Nye had realized that all this free food was intended for the poor—which didn't mean her, or George either. But she considered that since she was working here, she could share their meals—but just to be safe, she'd anonymously donated several thousand dollars. She supposed George had to be working too, even if she didn't know on what. It would be nice to think his employers were also contributing to the needy—she'd have to ask them if she got the chance.

She had to eat lunch, and she loved the cabbage soup here. If she took an extra long lunch break, so she could serve meals and clean up too, it also gave her the opportunity to study more of these twenty-first century denizens of New York City. Such as the woman who ran this place.

As good as the food they served was, it *could* be improved. But when Nye had suggested adding raw eggs and vinegar to the soup, that most sensible recommendation had not been well-received. Nye was still trying to analyze the woman's facial expressions as she'd listened to it. *She doesn't know what she's missing.*

Jeannie, one of the regulars, had yet to show up, and Nye hoped she hadn't been taken to the mental

Chapter 17

hospital again—their food wasn't nearly as good. If she asked, Bernie might know. Nye could try when she took her break to enjoy her own bowl of cabbage soup.

She dipped the ladle deep in the pot as the next man shuffled forward. Then her glasses were lighting up with facial recognition reports and microexpression analysis and bookmarks of previous video. She filled a bowl for him with a blank face and went on to serve the next person in line.

After Nye's first visit to this place and identifying 'George'—whose real name she still didn't know—she had taken the precaution of preprogramming certain subroutines into her glasses. Now that was paying off. She had found another person she'd encountered during her brief interaction with the FBI. She let her glasses keep a watch on both of them as she continued to serve the people in line, wondering what two federal agents were doing there disguised as the needy.

She waited until she'd served the last customer to ladle out a bowl of soup for herself. Grabbing the tray and a cup of coffee, she ran a more complicated analysis on the two men's behavior since they'd entered the building. By the time she'd sat down next to Bernie her glasses were displaying the results.

The two agents had been glancing at each other in a furtive fashion, which the report described as a mutual recognition with suspicion and gave a confidence rating of eighty-five percent. And it assigned a seventy-two percent likelihood to their being unaware of each other's reason for being there. A lower rating was given for the possibilities that they'd perceived each other as imposters but without recognition, or that there was some personal reason for the apparent discomfort with each other's presence.

Bernie turned and smiled at her. "Hi, Nye."

She smiled back. "Good afternoon, Bernie." Instead of asking about Jeannie, though, she became absorbed in slurping down her soup, and kept looking straight ahead.

The two federal agents sat a couple tables ahead of her, one to either side. Her glasses kept both men in view and displayed the video of each in the center of her lenses. The new one was trying to watch her out of the corner of his eye—but George was paying more attention to the new arrival. Considering her options as she drank her coffee, Nye came to a conclusion. She needed to confront them if she wanted to sort out what was going on.

She stood and marched down the center aisle to position herself between the two men and swiveled her head back and forth to glare at them both. "You two clearly aren't here for the same reason. I don't understand what possible interest you could have in this place. Or is it me you want?"

Chapter 17

Both men sat with mouths gaping and eyes boggling as they stared at her, but 'George' was the first to recover. "What are you talking about? I'm here for the food. What else?"

Nye shook her head at him. "I recognize both of you." She pulled the relevant data up to make sure of her facts. "I saw you two months ago, on the fifteenth of May in the Javits building, walking down a corridor on a certain floor. But I wasn't able to see your ID." She turned to face the other one. "And on that same day, you were the one who'd followed me to Times Square. You were even—"

She stopped because he'd finally shut his mouth and then opened it again right away, to blurt something out. "The *pizza* is sour. The pizza *is* sour."

Since they never served pizza, Nye was standing there trying to figure out what he'd meant by that a minute later when several men in suits charged into the place. Before she knew it, two of them were lifting her by the arms and hustling her from the building. They carried her around the corner and thrust her into the back of a big black van.

The men climbed in after her, and the van sped away, all before she had a chance to comment. "You should have presented your credentials. Or is it different for an undercover operation? I assume that's what that was intended to be, though I can't say you were doing a very good job of it."

Nye in the Soup

They didn't respond. Nye sighed—the last time this had happened, the agents had not talked much, but this time they weren't saying anything. Maybe because Special Agent Coulter wasn't there. "Aren't you allowed to talk when your boss is not around?" Apparently not, as the short ride stayed silent. She spent that time wondering if she'd broken any laws and whether she'd have to call Mr. Hollingsworth to help her out.

They took her to the same room as before. Coulter was waiting there, sitting in the very same chair. This time she took the initiative.

"What's the meaning of this? It should be clear to you by now that I'm not a terrorist. And what, by the way, are two FBI agents doing dressed up as the homeless and eating their food at that soup kitchen? I hope you're donating some money."

The man leaned back and smiled. "You're more confident than you were before. Are you aware that if we consider you a terrorist, we don't even have to let your lawyer know we're holding you? Much less allow you to speak to him."

Nye shook her head. "You're not a stupid man, Agent Coulter, so that's either an empty threat or a bullying tactic and an abuse of power, which I won't stand for. Either way, you want me to cooperate? Why not try telling me how I can help, and see how reasonable I can be?"

Chapter 17

Special Agent Coulter kept smiling at her without, as far as her glasses could detect, any microexpressions to indicate a particular attitude. "I could charge you with obstructing a federal investigation, Miss Walker. You were exposing an undercover operative, and that could get you some serious time in a federal prison, no matter who your lawyer is."

"That might be an interesting research project, to inspect the inner workings of a penitentiary. But it would interfere with my current studies, which I am still in the middle of, so I don't have a lot of time to waste. Now, I had not exposed either agent, and I was trying not to. But as they kept giving each other surreptitious looks, I thought I'd have to sort something out for them. They didn't seem to understand each other's presence."

Agent Coulter just sat there, staring, so she continued. "Since he had followed me in the past, I assume the one who just showed up today was watching me—if that's the case, I'd like to know why. And the other agent has been observing the soup kitchen for over three weeks now, and since he was already there before *I* showed up, I'd also like to know what possible reason the FBI could have for spying on the people there."

"Are you done?" He dropped his smile, shaking his head sadly at her. "I'm certainly not going to be telling you those things because you'd like to know.

It's enough for you to know that you disrupted our operation, and that we take a very dim view of that."

Nye snorted. "You should be blaming your people, not me. Their shifty behavior was the problem with your operation, or operations. Are you so disorganized that you can't coordinate between different investigations?"

Agent Coulter gave her a wry grin. "Since I was in charge of both operations, it wasn't a question of coordination. I'm not surprised you made the man who'd followed you in the past, but I must admit to being curious how you spotted the other man as being a federal agent."

"Oh, that." Nye waved her hand and blinked to bring the relevant data back up. "The last time you brought me here, two months ago, when I was walking to the elevator, I saw him down one of the hallways, wearing a suit and walking with other men in suits—and none of them wore a visitor's badge. So, they must have been federal agents."

Nye hoped she had not gotten those agents into trouble, but she had to impress Special Agent Coulter. Of course, she had been oblivious to all of that at the time, but anything her glasses recorded could be searched, even identifying profiles at a distance. And her glasses recorded everything.

"You must have a very good memory for detail, Miss Walker. Photographic?"

Chapter 17

Nye nodded. She supposed that term accurately be applied. "I can recall every detail of anything I've actually seen." If she'd been wearing her glasses at the time, of course.

"Well then, perhaps there's something you can help us with." Agent Coulter stretched out his hand and another agent stepped forward and passed him a plastic bag. He slid it across the table so she could get a good look. "Do you recognize this watch?"

It was one of their Travel devices, and again Nye was glad she'd taken to leaving her own in her room safe. There were ten of the watches altogether, and she wondered whose it was and how it had ended up in the hands of the FBI. "I can't identify one specific watch out of however many identical watches there must be." With that statement out of the way while it was still true, Nye casually flipped the bag without looking directly at—but her glasses saw. The designation on the back was H—6, Kirin's watch.

He took the bag back and opened it, withdrawing the watch and pressed one of the buttons. Then he held it up in front of her face. "Do you know who this person is? Have you ever seen them before, or can you give us any idea who they might be?"

She blinked as she stared at a picture of Samantha displayed on the watch screen. Supposedly her fellow researcher was off gallivanting around somewhere in time with Bailey. According to Anya.

Nye wondered if this had something to do with why her team leader had been hanging around her rooms at the Ngaio for the past couple of weeks. It would be best, Nye decided, to only answer the last of Agent Coulter's questions.

"I'm sorry, but I can't tell you who she is or anything that might identify her for you."

"So you have no idea why a professional hit man would be carrying a watch with her picture on it?"

"No." She could certainly answer that one with the truth. *What has Sam been up to?* And Anya always complained about Nye getting herself in trouble. "But I don't understand why you would think I had an idea about such a thing."

He looked for a moment as if he would tell her, but then he shook his head. "We had our reasons to suspect there might be a connection to you."

It had to be Anya. Somehow Anya was involved with all this, but clearly Agent Coulter wasn't going to tell Nye. So she would have to drag the details out of her team leader.

"You see, I cooperated. Now, is there anything else you wanted to ask me?"

"No, Miss Walker, that's all for now. But I expect I'll be seeing you in the future."

Nye wanted to get back to her research, but she needed to find Anya and have a little chat first.

Chapter 18
I Can't Help Myself

July 15th, 2003 Downtown Manhattan

ANYA loitered in Foley Square across from the entrance to the Javits Federal Building. She looked at the trees in full blossom and glanced occasionally at the locator screen on her watch to make sure Kirin's helper device wasn't being moved. If the authorities decided to take the watch someplace else, she wanted to know—that might be her only opportunity. So far she hadn't been able to devise a plan to get it out of the FBI's field office.

Once in a while she'd look at the people passing in and out through the main doors, hoping for inspiration. She'd been at this for two weeks and hadn't found any. Then she saw Nye exit the building.

Anya stood and stared at the girl as Nye strolled away, oblivious to her leader's presence. *What was she doing in there?* Nye was heading north, swiveling her head back and forth as she went, but not appearing to pay attention to anything. Anya hurried to follow. Whatever had brought the girl to the Federal Building, it could provide the opportunity Anya needed to obtain Kirin's watch. She needed to talk to the girl anyway about getting herself into trouble, and she could find out what the current mess was all about, and see if there was any way to make use of it. There had to be.

Ignoring Hollingsworth's admonition to let him see what *he* could do to retrieve the watch, Anya had lingered outside the Whitaker Building to follow the police investigation. She'd tracked the device from there back to the local precinct and later to the Federal Building. It had been the lawyer, however, who had discovered that the case, and the evidence, had been taken over by the FBI.

He'd said he didn't want to tip anyone off to the interest they had in the watch and had been careful with his inquiries, but he had found out the mystery man with Kirin's device had been a hired killer. So Anya didn't feel too upset about being inadvertently responsible for his death—but it did complicate any idea of trying to get the watch back. If she could just get close enough, she might be able to Travel it away

Chapter 18

from the FBI. But getting into the secure building to get that close would be a challenge. Nye had been in there, though.

Anya continued stalking after the girl, who was walking in the direction of their rooms at the Ngaio. Anya would tackle her there. And if whatever mess the girl had gotten into didn't present an opportunity to get Kirin's watch, Nye would have to lend Anya her own helper device. With a second device to multiply the range, it might be possible to Travel Kirin's watch away from the FBI from outside the building. That would leave the simple task of tracking it down with the locator app.

With everybody else gone, the only other device Anya could borrow would be Tate's, but she couldn't bring herself to tell him what she'd done. But if Nye was in trouble, then Anya wouldn't need to give her any explanation for why she wanted her watch.

She followed her back to the hotel without difficulty, but hesitated before the door to Nye's suite. It wouldn't be easy confronting her nominal assistant, not when Anya hadn't actually been supervising the girl for a long time. When she'd prepared her mind and summoned her authority, she knocked.

Nye opened the door just a moment later, blinking furiously at Anya and somehow making her feel at a loss. Then the girl stepped back from the door. "Come in, Cousin Anya."

I Can't Help Myself

Anya took a deep breath and made herself walk in, following Nye to the sitting room. As soon as the girl turned back to look at her, Anya took the initiative. "I don't know what you've gotten yourself involved in, but I saw you leaving the Federal Building downtown, and you need to tell me what's been going on."

"And what were you doing hanging around outside the Federal Building?"

"I'm your leader, remember, and I asked *you* a question. Look at all the trouble I've had to get you out of, and now this—whatever this is. What is it?"

Nye shook her head. "*I'm* not in any trouble at the moment, Leader. The FBI just wanted to ask me some questions—but they've been following me and they have probably been following you, so I doubt it was a good idea to skulk behind me all the way back here."

Anya paused. "I didn't think you saw me. And I wasn't skulking."

"Whatever you call it—you probably looked suspicious to them—you did to me. Do you want me to run the video through my kinesics analyzer and see how it describes your body language?"

"I don't think that's necessary. And you haven't yet said why federal agents should be following you —or me, for that matter." Anya tried to pull herself together. "Why would they?"

Chapter 18

Nye cocked her head. "That's what I wanted to ask you. What have *you* been up to? Something to do with Samantha?"

"Samantha?"

"They showed me one of our Travel devices and it was displaying a picture of her. At least it wasn't a leader device, the way they were handling it. Somehow they've connected the watch to you, which was why they asked me about it."

"The watch?" Anya felt a little light-headed. "I think I'll just sit down, if you don't mind."

Nye nodded brusquely and sat down in an armchair and waited for Anya to follow suit. "I hope you can explain what's going on, Leader."

"I suppose I ought to tell you about it." She certainly wasn't going to talk about trying to save John or how she'd mucked that up. "It's Kirin's watch. It must be. According to Sam it had gone missing."

"It is Kirin's—I saw the designation on the back. It can't Travel on its own, at least, but if the authorities start taking a particularly close look at it..."

Anya sighed. "Which they will, eventually. It's why I've been trying to figure out how to get it away from them."

"But how did they get it in the first place?"

"Apparently it had fallen into the hands of some kind of assassin—I don't have any idea how—and he was killed, and the watch was on the body."

Nye squinted. "They told me about the hit man and little else. But how can they connect the watch to you?"

Anya couldn't lie. "I saw the blip on my locator screen and got close enough to see the corpse. But I couldn't get near enough to take the device. The police saw me on surveillance video, though, and after that business with the professor's watch..."

"I'm surprised they didn't haul you in."

"The New York police were suspicious, and they had some questions, but the video proved I didn't go near the man, and I had Mr. Hollingsworth running interference for me."

"Well, the FBI have the device now. And I'd be surprised if *they* didn't pull you in for questioning, even with Hollingsworth for your attorney. They've got a reputation for tenacity that I think is earned."

Anya felt her shoulders droop but rallied. "Suppose they do. There's no evidence to show I did anything wrong, and it would give me the chance to use my own watch to Travel Kirin's out of the building."

Nye's mouth actually popped open as she stared back. "Have you lost your senses, Leader?"

"What do you mean?"

"If they actually brought you in to the New York field office, the agents would search you, and they'd find your watch. Then they'd have hard evidence of a connection between you and this hit man. They'd

Chapter 18

also have your leader device, and we'd all be in a lot of trouble."

Anya felt sweat suddenly break out on her forehead. *What's happening to me?* She kept her cool and her head in crises, of which she'd been through many—that's who she was—so why was she losing it now? It had all started with her foolish idea of Traveling back to the summer of two thousand to try and save the professor. She'd known she shouldn't even try, and yet she'd gone ahead anyway.

Everything had gotten progressively worse after that, to the point where now she had to sit and listen to a lecture from one of her assistants. Removing a handkerchief from her pocket, she wiped the sweat from her brow, then held her head in her hands.

Anya needed to get a grip. Otherwise she would only create more problems. That meant she needed to stop trying to do anything until she'd gotten help for herself. Then she realized something.

Lifting her head, she asked. "If the FBI brought you in for questioning—that's how you know all this, isn't it—did they take your watch?"

Nye shook her head. "I leave it here in the room safe, because I don't need it when I'm out doing my research."

"Of course. You learned that lesson from your brief stay in the psychiatric hospital. You've grown quite a bit since we started this." And she felt Nye needed to mature more still. That could come with greater responsibility.

Anya smiled at Nye, then took the leader device off her wrist. "It looks like the only way to retrieve Kirin's watch will be to Travel it from a distance. I'd planned to borrow your watch to multiply the effect of mine, but since you seem to know so much about how the FBI does things, perhaps you should be the one to recover the device."

Nye looked at the watch Anya was holding with a blank expression. "What do you mean by that?"

"I'm not making you leader. But your own device is useless for Traveling Kirin's out of FBI hands so I'm lending you this one. And giving you the job of getting it back." *I certainly shouldn't be trying to handle that task myself, but it's got to be done.*

The girl hesitated for a long moment, staring at the watch before reaching out to take it. "Alright. I accept the challenge. But what about Sam?"

"What about her?"

"A professional killer had that watch—with her picture on it. I don't know why or what that's about, but the FBI might. Anyway, I don't like it."

Anya sighed. "There's nothing we can do about Samantha. We don't have any idea where in space and time she might be. We'll be blessed if we recover Kirin's watch and avoid a complete catastrophe. But if you think you can solve that problem too—"

Chapter 18

Nye shook her head. "I'm just curious. I wish I had enough time to do all the research I want to do, and now I've got to retrieve this errant device. That may not be as simple as you're making it out. If it's been what—two weeks or more since that watch has been worn by a living person? It might not have the charge it needs to create a sympathetic field to Travel at all."

Anya sighed again, deeply. "I'd thought of that, but surely it's worth a try. If it doesn't work, I hope you can think of something else that will actually get the job done." She was especially glad she'd passed on this responsibility now. It would be a relief to go back to Tate and the house in Chickadee.

"And what if it did Travel, while some FBI agent happened to be holding it?"

She could not stop a tiny groan escaping. "Then what *will* you do?"

Nye lifted her eyes to the ceiling. "I'm going to have to examine this dilemma from a lot of different angles. One thing I'll have to do is see Mr. Hollingsworth and ask how he might be able to help."

Anya nodded. "I've already talked to him about it, and he's looking into it."

Nye lowered her gaze and peered at Anya's face. "I don't suppose he recommended skulking around the Federal Building?"

"No, I was definitely acting against advice."

Nye nodded. "That's what I thought. Well, Mr. Hollingsworth has been quite useful, and we're paying him already—so I'll consult with him right away. What will you do?"

Anya smiled again. "I'm going to go back to my own research. It might get boring, but right now I would be happy with boring. You can still call me if you need my help with anything though."

"I will. Speaking of which. I need more time—why don't you let me take the slow path? I can stay here year-round and get more work done."

"I have no objection. But since I'm lending you my leader device, you'd have to give that back first."

"Or at the end of the summer, if I haven't yet recovered Kirin's watch, I could come to Chickadee to Travel you and Tate to the following summer. And then return on my own."

"We'll see, Nye. You've got a lot of work to do—focus on that first." Anya was still this girl's leader, and that was probably more than she could handle. It was a good thing Tate never needed her help.

Chapter 19
An Inside Job

March 6th, 2013 Burnt Ash, Virginia

VERITY was going through the jumble of morning mail on her desk when she felt herself being kicked in the stomach. Or maybe it had been a punch. The child inside her had started moving around early in her pregnancy, according to the doctor. Now it was getting rambunctious. He or she seemed as anxious to get out as Verity was to have the baby—and there were three months to go yet. They were both going to have to learn some patience.

Her mixed feelings on learning that Turner had gotten her pregnant on their wedding night had given way to pure wonder and joy at the life growing on the inside of her. That had gradually become mitigated by the increasing discomfort, and supposedly the worst was yet to come. She could blame Turner for all of that, rather than the child.

Thinking about her husband always started her speculating, at least with the corner of her mind not occupied with her job—which right then was sorting the office mail. Some of it was junk mail to be recycled, most of it was routine business for her to handle, and a few choice pieces got through to Mr. Hollingsworth. She knew a lot more about her employer after working here for several months than she'd ever known about her own husband. For the umpteenth time, Verity wondered if she had rushed into matrimony. *Wedded bliss would be inapt.*

She had been so captivated by the man from the first time they met that she'd resolved to hook, then land Turner with a steady determination that she'd only applied to her work before. And to her astonishment, it had worked. She'd captured his interest almost too easily, he'd stubbornly resisted any real intimacy, and then suddenly there'd been the whirlwind courtship and wedding and—

Witness where it had left her. She had a bun in the oven and a missing husband. Who was a time-traveler from the future, and that was the only concrete detail she knew about his life. She thought she knew his character, and that he had good genes. If it weren't for those two things, she could cry when she

Chapter 19

thought of the child she was carrying—whose father was either lost somewhere in time, or dead.

Verity took a deep breath and reminded herself that there were people with bigger problems. Karat for one—the woman's husband had been murdered and she was hiding out with a new identity and newborn child. Verity had quite a lot to be grateful for, like this job. With a sigh she stopped thinking about herself, took Mr. Hollingsworth's small pile of mail, and walked into his office holding it all atop her protruding belly.

The lawyer looked up and watched her drop his mail into the antique wooden inbox on his desk and shook his head. "It's a good thing I gave up my office in Manhattan. It was too classy there to have a secretary so obviously pregnant—I would've had to insist you take maternity leave."

"You're a dinosaur, sir, living in the last century. I'd have had to sue."

He ran his finger down his mustache as he considered that. "You'd have had to get another lawyer, of course. Conflict of interest. Which also applies if you decide to sue Turner for abandonment. Technically I represent him as well. Still no word?"

As if she would've failed to mention it if she had heard from her husband. "Not a peep. And I'm sorry to disappoint you, but I've no intention of suing anyone. I wouldn't give you the satisfaction, and I

An Inside Job

have all I'd want from Mr. Belue already." *And then some.* She caught that snide thought, then tossed it into her mental trash can. It wasn't true. But Verity found herself becoming more snarky as her pregnancy advanced. At least that was what she blamed it on.

Hollingsworth shook his head. "I suspect, Mrs. Belue, that you know much more about Turner and the rest of those Travelers' Trust people than you let on. Can you really not know where he is or what he might be up to?"

She sighed and shifted to stand more comfortably. "I know a lot less than you'd think, sir. But any secrets aren't mine to share—theirs or yours—which brings me to your mail. Take that package sitting on your desk. The return address reads 'Secret Admirer', and you can confide in me about who she is, sir. I promise I won't tell your wife."

The lawyer snorted. "You and my wife are thick as thieves, so I know how far I'll trust that." Picking the package out of the pile, he read aloud the return address. "General Delivery, New York City."

"Of course it might be a bomb, sir. I'm sure you have plenty of enemies. Do you want me to run the package under some water in the sink?"

"I doubt if that would work with modern explosives. And all my enemies—thank you for that complement, by the way—would be more subtle."

239

Chapter 19

Verity sniffed. "Then I guess you'll have to take your chances and open it."

Hollingsworth raised his head and looked up at her. "I certainly wouldn't let you open it, not in your condition."

"Careful, sir. I might reconsider that lawsuit."

"That's your prerogative, certainly. But at least go across into the house and stay with my wife until I've seen if this is safe."

"Staying here to watch you open that is also my prerogative, sir. If it's from your girlfriend, you'd be advised not to have such things mailed here. Or not to work from home."

The lawyer grinned. "My wife already knows all the worst about me, and she's still here."

"And she'd likely appreciate it if you spent more time away from home then, wouldn't she, sir?" The former Mrs. Cooper had welcomed Verity replacing her as her husband's secretary.

"She's enjoying her time away from the office, I know. And dreading the day you do take maternity leave. You don't have to, you know. You can have the baby here if you want, as long as I'm not around at the time. Like women used to, you could just pop it out and get right back to work."

"You're a Neanderthal, sir, and I've got thirteen weeks before my due date—a bit early for Mrs. Hollingsworth to worry about working for you again."

Her employer squinted at her for a moment. "I suppose you must feel pretty confident this isn't really a bomb or you wouldn't be in here?"

Verity looked at the package he was holding. "It was sent by Express Mail, which would be unusual—unless they wanted to blow you up right away, or on a particular day." Of course she didn't believe there was any danger, or she would have removed herself to a safe distance. "And the Postal Service takes lots of precautions these days, sir. After everything."

"After all this fuss, would it be anticlimactic if I just opened it?" He took the sharp, gold-plated letter opener from its sheath on his desk, slit one end of the bulging envelope open, and dumped the contents out. What plopped onto his desk was a small, square box with rounded corners.

"Apparently your secret admirer is sending you some jewelry. Cufflinks? Or maybe she's not aware you have a wife, and that's a ring with a proposal? It looks like they got it from an outlet store, though. I would send it back if I were you."

Hollingsworth gave her a withering glare before returning his attention to the box. "Your condition must be impairing your sense of humor—it's getting worse and worse all the time. So if it's something so cheap I don't want to keep it, I can give it to you."

"I should sell it if you did, sir."

"Quite right, too."

Chapter 19

He returned the letter opener to its sheath, then pulled the box open. "Well, what do you know. It's a man's watch. Not my style, but it does seem a bit familiar. What do you think?" He took it out of its setting and handed it to her.

Verity couldn't hide her astonishment—a watch just like Turner's. She turned it over to see the inscription on the back. *H—6.* The one Matt had lent her for their disastrous trip, the one she kept stowed away in the back of her closet, that one was marked H—5. This could be its twin.

As she had been examining the watch, Hollingsworth had lifted the cardboard platform it had been sitting on and removed a couple items from the bottom of the box. One was a folded up sheet of paper which he held in one hand, the other a small object that he held out to her in his other palm. "And what, exactly, is that?"

"It's a USB drive, sir. For storing digital files— like for a computer. You wouldn't know about that, sir, being a dinosaur."

The lawyer unfolded the paper and read silently to himself before looking back at her. "This is from a contact of mine with the FBI. They ask me to see that watch handed over to Anya Walker, or another responsible party. That can be you, by the way, for the time being. As for the other thing, they only say it's something that will help Mrs. Silverman."

Verity cocked her head at him. "You have an informant inside the FBI?" That would be a real help to Karat. One of the things Hollingsworth had been able to discover was the fact that Senator Souseman had sicced the Feds onto Karat with an allegation of blackmail.

The lawyer gave her a funny look. "We've both got our secrets to keep, Mrs. Belue. Now, how do I go about finding out what's on that thing?" He nodded at the drive he was still holding out.

With a sigh she took it from him, and Hollingsworth refolded the letter and slipped it into his jacket's inside pocket. "I'll need to get my laptop." The lawyer refused to have a computer marring the antique glamour of his office.

He coughed discreetly and rose from his chair. "You'll do no such thing. I've kept you standing long enough. We'll adjourn to your office where you can sit down, and I'll stand looking over your shoulder. I just hope this is something I can use."

He followed her to the outer office, and she *was* glad to settle herself into the deluxe executive chair he'd gotten for her—and that was before Verity had discovered she was expecting. His wife's influence, no doubt.

As she waited for the laptop to boot up, she requested an update. "Are Karat and the baby managing alright? Have you heard anything recently?"

Chapter 19

Hollingsworth grunted. "I've not heard a thing. I set her up with that new identity to protect her, so I'm not going to risk getting in contact just to chat. She knows she should only get in touch in case of an emergency. So I assume they're both alright."

Verity shook her head and turned her attention back to her computer. She hesitated a moment before inserting the drive, but she'd set up her system to be as well-protected from viruses and every other potential threat as she could. And her employer did seem to trust his source in the FBI.

The window that opened showed only one large file. "It's a video, sir."

"Can we see it on that thing? If we can, is it safe to watch?"

Now he asks. "We can. I don't see how it could hurt just to look at it, but maybe I'd better avert my eyes in case." It might be something she didn't want to see.

"If you're worried about seeing something confidential, what good are you as my secretary?"

She double-clicked the icon.

What they both viewed then was a high-resolution video taken from the ground, looking up. Two men in dark suits walked to the edge of the roof of a multi-storied building—carrying a third man, seemingly unconscious between them. Then they casually tossed him over.

Verity and Hollingsworth both stared in silence for a long moment. Then she played the video again in full-screen mode and paused it where the face of that third man was clearly visible. "I've never seen a picture of Mr. Silverman. But you knew him."

The question was implicit, and of course he understood. "He's quite a bit older than the last time I'd seen him, but I recognize the man well enough."

"Now we know it was murder, and we can prove it, sir." She'd still had her doubts, but no more. She did wonder, though, who had taken that video, and how and why.

"Prove it to whom?" The lawyer started combing his mustache with his finger again, meaning he was deep in thought. "Those two men may be wearing sunglasses, but they can still probably be identified by facial recognition. If they are what they look like, though, that could be a problem."

"How? Do you recognize them too?"

"I know the type. They're spooks of some sort—CIA, military intelligence, or maybe an agency I've never heard of. It hardly matters."

Verity felt her jaw harden. "If government spies murdered Karat's husband, what can we do?"

"Senator Souseman made a mistake, I think, involving the FBI. Whatever agency those men came from who killed Silverman, I'm confident they were not acting officially."

Chapter 19

Verity looked up into his face. "Are you sure?"

Hollingsworth looked down into her eyes. "I do have some experience with these kinds of people. I know there are some bad apples among our national intelligence agencies who aren't too picky about the legality of what they do or who they do it for. Such as whoever Souseman had spying on his mistress."

"But if the FBI already had this video, why send it to you, unless they couldn't or wouldn't do something about it?"

"I don't think they did have this. But that explanation will have to wait. The point is—if the Bureau can identify those two men in the video, then I may be able to get them looking for a connection to Senator Souseman. That's where I think he erred. The FBI won't like it if they think he's been playing them for fools. They're not. They're slow, but they're tenacious, thorough, and methodical. All I have to do is get them started on the right trail."

Verity nodded. "I see. And at least if the FBI is investigating Souseman, they'll leave Karat alone."

"Probably, but it probably won't be safe for her to come out of hiding until the senator's been dealt with, and possibly not even then. That's why I gave her a new identity she should be able to live with as long as she needs to."

If it were Verity, and *her* husband who had been murdered like that, and she had a new child to care for, she doubted she'd want to go back to an old life that held only grief and danger. "Anyway, the important thing obviously is to use this video and your contact at the FBI to sic them on Souseman."

Hollingsworth grinned. "Indeed. I think being investigated by the Bureau would at least constrain him from trying too hard to find Mrs. Silverman—it also holds out the hope of justice for her husband."

Verity smiled back. "And you'll have to get back in contact with her to let her know. Finding out the truth will be important to her. And you can ask how the baby's doing."

"And I'll make sure to tell her about your condition as well. Now, we've got a lot of work to do, and you'll be doing most of it, so stop stalling."

"Yes, sir." First she'd help Hollingsworth fight this battle. Then it would be time to turn her focus to finding her husband and having her baby. She'd see which of those she accomplished first.

Chapter 20
Providence

September 11th, 1962 Pecos, Texas

TURNER felt like a new man. Bob had insisted on taking him to a decent hotel and pre-paying for a full week's stay. Then, while her husband had been arranging things with the desk clerk, Joy had slipped a hundred dollars into Turner's hand. "You'll need it to get back on your feet," she'd said.

And they had left him their phone number and address, asked him to call and let them know he was doing alright, and invited him to stop by to visit anytime. *Bless them.*

The first thing he had done after saying goodbye in the hotel lobby was to walk several blocks to find a discount store where he could purchase some new clothes. Not wanting to waste Joy's largesse, he was content buying anything inexpensive. And since he was in Texas, he chose blue jeans and denim shirts. His comfortable loafers were beyond repair, forcing him to give in and get a pair of cowboy boots, but he denied himself the matching hat. Aside from being an unnecessary expenditure, it would've been going one step too far. And looked plain silly.

Then he had returned to his hotel room to scrub himself raw getting all the sand and sweat off. And between the sun and the hot shower, his skin was so red that, added to the white shirt and blue jeans he had donned, he appeared aptly patriotic for Texas.

This new Turner left his room and made his way down to the small, dark dining room the hotel called a cantina. Here they likely served Mexican-inspired food tailored to the American palette. At least that was what he hoped.

Inside the dimly lit space, he saw no sign of any bartender or waiter, just one scrawny kid at the bar and all the tables empty. Turner might've gone out to search for someplace else to eat, but he'd walked enough for a while—he preferred to sit and relax for now—if he waited, presumably someone would appear, eventually. He sat down at one of those empty tables and picked up a menu to peruse.

"You'll be sitting there a long time if you're waiting on the waitress. She doesn't start 'til six."

Chapter 20

Turner glanced up from the menu to see the kid at the bar staring at him. "Is it too early for food?"

"That depends on whether you want something someone has to cook."

With a sigh, Turner stood and walked up to the bar, nodding at a seat one down from the kid before sitting there. The boy gestured with the beer bottle in his hand, then returned to staring at the stuccoed wall behind the bar—at which point, as if by a signal, the bartender walked out of an arch leading back to, presumably, the kitchen area. Then he started wiping down the counter.

Turner watched him for a minute before folding the menu and setting it down. "How about a bowl of guacamole and chips?"

The big man nodded. "And to drink?"

"A lime squash, please."

Turner slid a five-dollar bill across the counter, and the man returned a few minutes later carrying a giant basket of chips and a large bowl of fairly fresh-looking guacamole. The bartender mixed the drink and set it on a coaster. When Turner reached out to take the glass with his left hand as his right dipped a chip into the guacamole, he was conscious of the kid eyeing him.

"Your wristwatch."

Turner glanced over to see the kid staring. "So. What about it?"

The kid shook his head in wonder. "It looks digital. Is it?"

Turner stopped himself from pulling the cuff of his shirtsleeve down over the watch—it was too late. The kid had already seen it, and Turner didn't think digital watches existed yet. Not beyond prototypes, anyway. But that's what his watch was, in its way.

He nodded at the boy. "It's one of a kind—I'm a bit of an enthusiast."

Grabbing his chips and dip in one hand and his drink in the other, Turner began sliding off the bar stool to leave for a table—this was an awkward conversation, one he wanted to get away from—but the boy grabbed his sleeve and pulled him back.

"Wait. Eat here. I'd like to talk to you. Are you an electronics geek too? Do you know much about computers?"

Turner sat down with a sigh and took a sip of his drink before responding. "I know about integrated circuits." If he remembered right, that was the field for big innovations in this period. "I'm particularly interested in digital technology, as it relates to communications." Then he scooped a big hunk of guacamole up with a chip and stuffed his mouth to try to keep himself out of trouble.

"This is great. I'm studying electrical engineering myself. I'm on my way back to Dallas, to start a new semester."

Chapter 20

Turner smiled at the kid. "That *is* great. I hope you do well."

"My uncle got me an internship at Texas Instruments Central Research Lab for next summer. I can hardly wait. But what really interests me is computer programming."

"The TI labs were the birthplace of the integrated circuit—I think you'll be off to a great start."

The kid grinned. "My name's Brandt Keener by the way." He looked about to offer his hand, before noticing that Turner's were full.

"I'm Turner," he said by way of introduction.

"Just Turner?"

Turner just nodded as he stuffed another guacamole-loaded chip into his mouth.

"Cool. Are you one of those guys who's dropped out, gone off the grid?"

He supposed that description would fit his current circumstances, and shrugged.

"Let me guess—you went to Canada to avoid the draft? I don't blame you. The Korean War was one huge mess, but there's a bigger one on the horizon, in Vietnam. Maybe you'd have been better to stay in the North."

Turner occupied himself with washing down his food with a big gulp of lime squash.

Brandt held up his hand. "You don't want to say anything—I understand. Don't worry, I'm not going to narc on you. It doesn't bother me at all. I'd probably have to do the same thing—if my uncle wasn't a congressman."

Turner shook his head but didn't try to correct the kid. He needed some kind of explanation for his lack of identification, and this would do. He would have to say something which would seem to confirm this kid's misconception though. "I'll only say that I am constrained by conscience. I don't want to have to kill anyone."

"Sure, me too. It's not that I'm a coward or anything. The only killing I intend to do is in business. One day computers will run everything, and if I can come up with even one great idea, I'll have it made."

Swirling the liquid in his glass, Turner reflected on how he should respond. "A digital revolution—it will change everything, eventually."

The kid's eyes lit up. "You said it. It'll improve people's lives in every respect. The potential's enormous." He grinned at Turner from ear to ear. "Only I have to wait until I graduate for my dad to give me the money to start my own business. When I do, I'll come and hire you."

"That's nice kid, but I happen to be looking for a job for right now." He should probably head to Dallas like Brandt—maybe he could find a way into the burgeoning telecom industry. "But I'll look forward to seeing your name in the papers."

Chapter 20

Brandt couldn't stop grinning. "Have you got a car?" He continued as Turner shook his head. "I'll give you a ride into Dallas, then make some calls to line something up for you. If you *are* going to work for me, I want you to have the right experience. And anyone who can construct a digital watch by himself is someone I want working for me."

The kid still hadn't graduated, much less started a company, but already he was head-hunting. Turner shook his head in wonder, even as he winced to think of all the misconceptions he'd allowed the kid to grab hold of. But he couldn't tell the whole truth. At least he was capable of constructing a simple digital watch, of the sort the boy believed he was wearing.

"Thanks, I'd appreciate the help."

Brandt stopped grinning. "Only, school doesn't start until next week, so I'd planned to spend several more days here before I drove to Dallas. Can you wait that long?"

Turner nodded. After a few days in the desert, he was ready to wait as long as he needed to—and he might have to wait fifty years or more to see Verity. If he ever did see his wife again.

Maybe another Traveler would find Turner and help him make the trip faster, but he couldn't count on that. *But I can count on You.* He marveled at the way everything and everyone kept turning up at just the right time. Now Providence had positioned him where he needed to be to see the early stages of the digital revolution—the very aspect of history he had come back in time to study. Maybe even to be a part of it all himself.

He couldn't rely on this kid, though. He'd need to figure out how to establish a new identity for himself and bury 'Turner Belue'—so if he never made it back to the future, Verity would at least be a proper widow. And if he did make it back to her, she could always marry Turner Hope. Though if it took him a full sixty years to reach her, he'd be an old man, and she'd probably want to remain a widow.

Chapter 21
An Experiment in Hope

October 24th, 1918 Midtown Manhattan

PAGE slipped out into the corridor, looking in every direction to make sure Riggleston wasn't lying in wait—though she didn't think he could be up so early on a Sunday morning, not after all the drinking he had so obviously been indulging in the night before. All she saw was a maid at the other end of the hall—still, the woman might be a spy for him. Page didn't know what the man might've been up to. Not wanting to take a chance on ordering room service, she'd decided to go out and gather provisions to stockpile in her room. The fresh air would be nice too.

Turning and locking the door behind her, Page kept the maid in her peripheral vision as she placed a single hair securely in the crack between the door and the frame. When she returned, that would alert her if someone had gotten into her room. She hung the 'do not disturb' placard on the door to keep the maids out—so if she found anyone had entered her room, she would know it meant trouble.

She strolled down the corridor toward the door to the stairwell. That brought her closer to the maid and the realization that Page need not have worried about being spied upon. The woman was in far too much distress to even notice her—she continued to stand in front of the same door, wringing her hands and staring in apparent indecision.

Page's curiosity overcame her wariness. Walking the rest of the way down the hall, she saw another door with its 'do not disturb' sign up—but surely that couldn't be what was agitating the poor woman. Then she noticed the room number—412. *The same suite Matt has stayed in since that one time—*

A strange sensation buzzed at the back of Page's brain, but she forced her mind onto the maid. "Do you have some kind of problem here?" She'd automatically assumed the air of one who'd be an owner of this hotel in the future. "If the guest put that sign up, you really shouldn't even be thinking of going in there." *I had better reinforce that idea right now.* "I don't know what duties you have that might require you to enter the room, but..."

Chapter 21

The short, round, middle-aged maid spoke with a thick Italian accent. "No, you don't understand—listen!"

At first Page thought the woman meant to listen to her, and she waited patiently for the maid to offer an explanation. Then she heard a faint sound. Inclining her head toward the door, she was soon able to discern a distinct moan, but the building was too solid and the carpet too thick for the sound to carry much.

Page was suddenly seized with a conviction that Matt was in that room. Was it conceivable that he'd been struck by the same notion as she had, and that she had somehow missed him being right down the hall? *And he missed me.*

Confident that Page had heard the same sound, the maid started talking again. "I think he must be in pain, but when I knocked he didn't respond at all. We can't just leave him in there without help. But if he's sick, it might be the Spanish flu—in which case I shouldn't go in, but I'm supposed to call the health department. But in a nice hotel like this, rich gentlemen are not supposed to be sick with the flu, and men from the health department—the manager, he would not like them coming to the hotel."

Page could certainly understand the maid's hesitation now. It was a no-win situation for the woman, but that would give Page an opportunity to help

An Experiment in Hope

her out—and Matt at the same time. He would not want the authorities involved any more than the hotel manager.

Giving the maid a firm look, Page offered a suggestion. "I agree someone should check on him, but I wouldn't want you to get into trouble, so why don't you let me into the room to see what the situation is, and then maybe I'll have an idea how we can handle it. I believe I know the gentleman—Mr. Matt Walker, isn't it?"

"Yes, miss. I'm not really supposed to. But you promise you won't get me in trouble?"

Page nodded and pulled a twenty-dollar bill out of her reticule and pressed it into the woman's hand with a smile. "I promise. It's just between us." And that was far too big for a tip—the maid would recognize it for a bribe, and a substantial one. But then Page intended to start collecting allies against Riggleston.

Shaking her head, the maid took a key ring out of her apron pocket and selected one, presumably a master key of some sort, and unlocked the door before standing well back again. "If he's got the chain up, miss, you still won't be able to get in."

But he didn't. Page opened the door only wide enough to slip inside, then marched through the sitting room and into the bedroom beyond, where she saw Matt—sprawled on his back across the bed and

Chapter 21

fully-clothed. He was red and sweating, and moaning much louder than she'd suspected until she was inside. She felt herself overwhelmed by an unprecedented emotion.

Turning back, Page saw that the maid had mustered her courage and entered, at least as far as the other side of the sitting room. Page strode back toward the woman and shooed her out of the suite altogether. Standing in the doorway, with her hands on her hips, Page spoke with soft determination.

"He's clearly sick, but it's not the influenza. You don't have to worry, and nobody needs to notify the health department. Since I'm a friend of his, I'll see he gets the care he needs."

The maid hesitated. "But if something happens to the young gentleman, or if someone complains of the noise..."

Page shook her head. "I don't think anyone will even notice the noise. And I'm not going to let anything 'happen' to Mr. Walker." She pulled another twenty out and handed it to the maid with a nod. "I think we understand each other, yes?"

"Yes, miss." She looked past Page, in the direction of Matt's moaning, then brought the crucifix on a chain around her neck up to her lips, mumbling a prayer before heading off down the hall.

Backing up and closing the door, Page thought Matt could use any help he could get. He must have set up an account at the bank, but without identification that would be acceptable in this time, he was at a disadvantage if he had to deal with the contemporary authorities. Just like Page.

She stalked back to the bedroom and looked at Matt as he was lying there. He clearly needed medical attention. If it were simply a matter of calling a doctor, she wouldn't hesitate—but with everyone in the grip of a pandemic, he'd be quarantined. Given his lack of ID and the primitive state of medicine in this era, he would likely be packed in together with plenty of other patients in some overcrowded hospital, if he were fortunate. And they probably wouldn't be able to do any more for him than she could. They might even insist on quarantining Page as well—her assurances that she couldn't spread the flu wouldn't likely be believed.

While her bribe had worked on a maid who had not actually seen him, Page doubted she could pay a doctor enough to keep quiet once he had seen Matt. She certainly wouldn't be able to bribe some health department officials to turn a blind eye. She would just have to take care of him herself.

The main thing she, or anyone, could do to help Matt at this point was to make sure he got plenty of fluids. She remembered a bit of Anya's lecture concerning treatments available in the past—which was generalized information pertaining to the twentieth

Chapter 21

and twenty-first centuries and incomplete, for what that was worth. Acetaminophen might alleviate his fever, but Page didn't think that was readily available, if at all, yet. A bath in cold water would be the next best thing.

Well, he needed to be gotten out of those sweat-stained clothes and cleaned up anyway. Page would have liked to hire someone to do that job for her, but she had taken a risk already with that maid—it had been necessary, but she wouldn't take more chances unless she had to. Besides, anyone she hired to help her would also be exposed to the flu, and she didn't want that on her conscience.

She stepped closer to the bed and wrinkled her nose at the smell. Leaning over, she reached behind to grab Matt under the armpits, but his dead weight was too much for her. So she took hold of the duvet under him and slid it, and him with it, off the sheets and onto the floor with a great thump. It was hard work, but she managed to drag the Matt-laden quilt across the carpet and into the bathroom, right up to the rim of the wide wooden platform that surrounded the tub. There she paused and considered how to get him in. She decided that because the bedspread and his clothes would all need to be cleaned anyway, she might as well soak them now.

So continuing to use the counterpane as a moving inclined plane, she stood in the tub and dragged

An Experiment in Hope

and pulled at the bottom end of the quilt and shifted position several times until she'd managed to get all of him in, then turned on the cold water. Collapsing against the wall, she sat down on the side of the tub to relax while it filled.

Thankfully Page was still alert enough as she sat there to notice that Matt was wearing the professor's watch. It might not have been properly fixed, but it never would be if she let it soak. She took the device off his wrist and leaned back again, listening to the water rushing into the tub and trying to think about the things she could do to help him. It was good that he was delirious with fever and next to unconscious, but not for what came next—getting him to drink.

She wondered how long he had been like this. If he'd come through when she had Traveled, he could not have been here one whole day. That was a short time to get this sick. Maybe he'd taken the slow path for three years to get here. He might've been ill for days. Neither explained why he hadn't shown up on her locator screen though.

It became an effort to keep her eyes open while she watched the water level rise. When the tub was mostly full, she turned off the tap and turned to the difficult job of finding a way to get him to drink water. First she lifted him enough so the rim of the tub propped his head up. She checked to make sure he was stable and wouldn't slip under and drown, then

Chapter 21

she went and got a glass and filled it with water out of the sink.

This time she sat on the end by his head, pressing the lip of the glass against his lips and forcing a sip at a time gently down his throat. Fluids into his system and soaking in cold water should help him a lot with the fever. It would also loosen all that sick and sweat that clung to him and his clothes and the quilt. She had done what she could for the moment, but she didn't like to leave him alone like this—with a sigh she sat in the less than comfortable chair that sat against the bathroom wall, leaned her head back—and promptly nodded off. When she woke with a start sometime later, she was glad to see he was still alive and breathing.

Page pressed her hand to his forehead. He was burning up—no better as far as she could tell, but at least he didn't seem to have gotten any worse. She really wanted to freshen herself up more than anything, but first she had to do all she could for Matt. And right now that meant draining the dirty water. So she unblocked the drain and let it all slowly run down and away.

Then she took a deep breath to gather her energy for what came next—she maneuvered the sodden bedspread out from under him bit by bit. Wringing it out took a lot of her strength, and even more dirty water washed down the drain. She folded the damp duvet and laid it across the far side of the tub. Her next job was getting Matt out of his clothes.

Half-averting her eyes, she slowly stripped the water-logged garments off. She wrung those out as well and tossed them on top of the folded bedspread before reaching to take one of the large, clean, plush towels from the cupboard by the tub and draping it over him for decency. Then she turned the tap, and clean, cold water flowed into the tub again.

Page took a washcloth and soaked it in cold water and laid it across Matt's forehead before leaning back to watch the water level rise. Finally she shut the tap off and left the bathroom. She'd done everything she could for him for the time being—now she needed to take care of herself.

Checking her watch, she was amazed at how little time had actually passed. It should still be early enough that she need not worry about running into Riggleston. She looked out into the hallway and saw the coast was clear. Leaving the door to Matt's suite unlocked and the 'do not disturb' sign in place, Page scurried down the corridor to her own rooms.

Seeing no one had been in, she entered her own suite with a sigh of relief. She refreshed herself and grabbed everything she thought she might need and left again, not forgetting to reset her little alarm. A bare half hour had passed by the time she returned to Matt's room and found nothing had changed.

Chapter 21

After she'd checked on Matt's condition, she sat down in one of the comfortably stuffed armchairs in the sitting room and took the telephone receiver off the hook and asked the hotel operator to connect to the store she'd shopped at only yesterday—it felt as if it had been a week. She told them she needed her new clothes, the ones she'd ordered yesterday, to be delivered to a different room—Matt's room, though she didn't mention that aspect. She wouldn't leave him on his own until he was well again.

Page didn't know where Matt's clothes might be —she had looked around his rooms but hadn't been able to find any besides what he'd been wearing. He had worn a different suit when she'd seen him at the parade, so he must've gone shopping since, whether she'd Traveled him forward from nineteen fifteen to yesterday or he'd taken three years going down the slow path. But if he'd been here that long he should have a *few* outfits. Either way, he'd need something to put on once he was feeling better—more than that complementary robe hanging in the bathroom.

Page wouldn't allow herself to consider the possibility that he wouldn't improve. But she would let him shop for his own clothes then—all *she* would do was have the suit he had been wearing cleaned so he had something decent to put on.

Page pulled one of the comfortable chairs from the sitting room into the bathroom, then sat next to

An Experiment in Hope

Matt. She managed to force him to sip down some more water, but his fever still raged. At some point her delivery arrived, and after that another delivery, of clothes Matt had apparently ordered for himself. Once she'd dealt with all that, she ordered room service.

Page had never been able to get out and get supplies, and now she was hungry. Because the request came from Matt's room, hopefully Riggleston would not hear of it, but of course the hotel staff must have suspected something, so he might. If he discovered she was sharing a suite with another man, maybe he would lose interest in her. Another thing she hadn't had time for was thinking of a way to deal with him.

Now, washed and fed and wearing new clothes, she had a break to consider it, but she couldn't with Matt lying there in the bathtub—and possibly dying. He seemed to have gotten worse as the day had progressed. Despite her efforts, his fever had not gone down, and his breathing had become horribly shallow. He wasn't moaning anymore.

Page left his side and went to stare out the bedroom window in frustration. The sun had started to set, and the eastern exposure was already dark—she could see her reflection in the glass, a ghostly image across the city's skyline. A ghastly vision actually, as her appearance was suffering under the strain. But as she gazed out, she stopped seeing that and turned

Chapter 21

her eyes inward to inspect her memory. *There must be something there that will help.*

Her mind sped back across the lectures and orientations, the instructions, discussions, and preparations—surely Anya had dropped some snatches of medical wisdom along the way, something applicable to Page's present predicament. But what finally came unbidden to her brain were some words from the professor as he'd strayed off onto one of his tangents.

Page had trained her memory, learned to discipline her thoughts and focus her attention. And she used that to recall every scrap she'd heard.

Research Leader Harold had asked some stupid question about catching diseases from the natives—the professor had glared hard at both him and Page but not Anya, who must've escaped because she already knew what he was about to say. Then he went on and on about how humans of the past had quite inferior immune systems. He'd reviewed a vast host of diseases that had plagued people in the past—in a way that had not reassured Harold in the slightest.

The professor had specifically referred to the influenza pandemic of the early twentieth century, because of how it had hit the young and healthiest the hardest. "Viruses can be clever devils," he'd said.

The pressure of her emotions began to interfere with her focus, so Page stopped and took a few deep breaths, letting her mind grow calm and rested before she allowed the memory to return.

The professor had shaken his head, presumably at the viruses. "Even back then, the immune system was a marvelous thing. But it often didn't work the way it was supposed to. That strain of influenza got itself a fighting chance by triggering a massive overresponse from that incredible immune system. The healthy young human body would release a flood of antibodies that had not been properly programmed to target the virus and would target the very tissues damaged by the flu. Giving the virus a chance to get lost in the crowd, as it were.

"So the deadly danger was not the flu itself, but those very antibodies meant to protect the individual. In their frenzied attack, they would trigger a cytokine storm that perpetuated the body's assault on itself. Various organs, particularly the lungs, would begin to shut down, and a lot of people died. But not many of those with weakened immune systems who only had to fight the flu. Rest and fluids and maybe ice to bring down the fever were usually enough."

So Matt had two serious problems—the influenza virus and his body itself—with his own antibodies being the greater threat. If only he had Page's superior system, with lymphocytes that would not be deceived. Her B-cells and T-cells could handle the flu virus with one protein chain tied behind their backs

Chapter 21

—but Matt's stupid cells were fighting the wrong enemy. If only there were something Page could do to fix that. But her own immune system was an inheritance, and she couldn't give it to him.

What she might be able to do, though, was give him the antibodies that could properly target the flu virus. Once the virus had entered her body—and it might have done so already—she knew her superior immune system would immediately identify the intruder and start pumping out the correctly calibrated antibodies to eliminate it. Those proteins would be perfectly matched to the same antigens along the surface of the virus' molecules in Matt's body. So all she had to do was make sure she was infected to get her super-lymphocytes into action and find a way to transfer her immunoglobulin into his blood.

It would at least take care of the virus. But there was nothing she could do to stop the cytokine storm ravaging Matt's body. While her own immune system would recognize malfunctioning antibodies belonging to her own body, and destroy them just the same as it would take care of an alien invader, there would be no way it could know whether Matt's cells were acting properly or not. But she had hope—that if the virus was eliminated from his body, maybe his immune system would realize it could stop fighting—that it would cease killing him by waging a war on the wrong front.

An Experiment in Hope

Whether it would work or not, that was the only thing she could do now. She went back to sit at the tub where she could look down into his fevered face and think about the easiest way to make certain she was infected with the virus. This wasn't exactly how she had imagined their first kiss.

Page leaned over and gently pressed her lips to his. His eyelids fluttered and his lips pressed back, but that wasn't enough to be sure. So she eased his mouth open and slid her tongue against his all the way to the back of his throat. He was far too out of it to be aware, and far too sick for it to be anything but unpleasant for her. But she had to give the flu plenty of time to try attacking her.

She held his head and continued the contact as long as she could, because not only did she need the virus to attack her, but in sufficient strength for her immune system to really start pumping out the immunoglobulin. At last she pulled away and allowed herself to relax and catch her breath. That had been the easy part.

It shouldn't take long for her body to begin the process of churning out millions of little killers prepared to go after the influenza virus like trained assassins. Then the problem would be to get as many of them onto the battlefield in Matt's body as possible, and as quickly. That would be the hard part, because she didn't have the training or the equipment

Chapter 21

for a blood transfusion, or to try isolating the immunoglobulin from her blood and injecting it into him.

So after gathering her energy, she had to gather her courage. This would not only be unpleasant—it would probably make her sick. She deliberately bit down hard on her tongue, felt the blood running in her mouth, and kissed him again, her stomach turning over as she did so. Once again she also swapped fluids with him for as long as she was able to. That reminded her of a fad from the fifties, or maybe the sixties—kissing marathons.

She had intended to have Matt help her experiment with one of those, as part of her research, but now she was having second thoughts.

Her strength waning, Page pulled away again to rest. By now, the antibodies she'd generated would be doing their best to destroy all the influenza they could find, and she'd done what she could for Matt. Next was the hardest part of all—waiting.

Chapter 22

Unscheduled Appointments

October 25th, 1918 Midtown Manhattan

MATT woke with a crick in his neck and a beating in his head. He pried his eyes open and found himself lying in a damp bathtub and covered with a wet towel. He thought he'd been too delirious to get out of bed even, but apparently he'd managed to make it into the bathroom, undress, and soak himself. And now his fever had broken.

Climbing over the edge of the tub, he groaned as his muscles protested trying to stand upright. Then he looked around. He saw his watch lying on top of the chest against the wall and was relieved that he'd thought to take it off before immersing himself. He couldn't see his clothes anywhere around though.

Chapter 22

Matt must have shed his clothes in the bedroom before staggering in here. He took a clean, dry towel and wrapped it around his waist before going to see in what state he'd left the rest of the suite. The outfit he'd been wearing wasn't there, but a whole new set of suits hung in the closet—the hotel staff must have let in the delivery of the new garments he'd ordered and hung everything up for him. They had probably taken his old clothes to be laundered. Now that was service.

The pounding came again, louder, and he realized it wasn't in his head but at the door. He hadn't checked the time on his watch, but the sun was shining through the window so it must've been morning. He didn't know how long he had been out of it. Nor could he recall how long he'd paid for when he had checked in. Maybe they'd come to chuck him out.

The knocking came again, more insistent. Matt yelled out, "I'm coming." But first he had to dress, and he didn't have time to put on a suit. Despite his aching body, he stumbled back to the bathroom and grabbed the fuzzy robe that hung there and hurried back to the sitting room. But someone was already inserting a key and opening the door.

A man who must've been the manager pushed it all the way to the wall and then stepped back, allowing two other men to enter—or try to.

Matt stood in the way. "What's this about?"

The bigger of the men swiftly brought a mask to his mouth and stepped forward into Matt's personal space. "I'm with the New York City Health Department. Are you aware that if you're sick you are required to be checked out to see if you have the Spanish flu? But you haven't reported your illness." The bureaucrat turned his head to look at the small man standing behind him and carrying a black bag. "He looks red and flushed, doesn't he?"

Matt bristled. "That would be because I just got out of the bathtub and ran in here to get the door—because someone was pounding on it. I'm not sick." At least, he was pretty sure he wasn't ill anymore.

"The doctor will still have to examine you. We had a report." That must've been whoever brought those new clothes to his room. "If he certifies you as not contagious, fine. Otherwise we may have to isolate the entire hotel."

Standing behind the two men, the hotel manager blanched. Even the doctor looked uncomfortable about it. And then into that sudden silence, a familiar voice rang out. "If he's looking flushed, it must be because he's running late."

Page appeared in the corridor behind the three men, looking amazing in a vivid blue dress that only highlighted her glorious red hair. Which made Matt remember a fever dream he'd had—of Page kissing him, at length. He blushed, but you couldn't hold a

Chapter 22

man responsible for his dreams—especially if they'd been fever-induced delusions. She ignored the others and squinted at his bathrobe. No doubt she disapproved.

Matt grinned. "Talk about a sight for sore eyes." But the rest of him was still sore.

"And you promised to take me to tea, but look at you. You're not even dressed yet."

"Give me ten minutes, and I'll be downstairs in the dining room, looking sharp." He glanced at the men standing between them and sighed dramatically. "Actually, you'd better make it twenty. I have to satisfy the doc I'm not sick first."

Page glared at him. "I'll give you five minutes." Then she swept her glare over the other three men. "You gentlemen had better not cause him to be one minute late." With a nod to herself, she turned and disappeared down the hall.

With a sigh, Matt backed up to allow the doctor and the bureaucrat into his rooms. The hotel manager, meanwhile, had discreetly faded away—to placate Page if he was smart. The doctor, now donning his own mask, maneuvered Matt down into a sitting room chair and began taking his temperature—this he followed with listening to Matt's heart and lungs, staring down his throat, and peering under his eyelids. The examination took more than five minutes, and Page would blame Matt.

The doctor turned to the bureaucrat, who stood behind him and had been looking over his shoulder. "He might've been up all night, partying. He's worn out, but he's not sick. He certainly doesn't have the flu."

The health department official clenched his jaw. "You're sure about that? If you make a mistake with a thing like this..."

Now it was the doctor who turned beet red, but with anger, not embarrassment. "Are you questioning my evaluation? You're the one who dragged me here on a wild goose chase." The doctor proceeded to bundle his stethoscope and other equipment into his black bag and walk out, without another word to the other man. The bureaucrat followed him out, in similar silence.

Neither of them had bothered to even glance at Matt again, much less apologize, but he didn't care. He just sprang into action and dressed as fast as his aching muscles could move. Hurrying back into the bedroom, he selected a lightweight blue pin-striped suit and put on the loafers he'd managed to take off before he'd fallen into bed last night. He forsook the tie, but darted into the bathroom to grab his watch. And when he looked at the time, he realized that it had not been the previous night he'd fallen sick, but the night before. Page must've visited the bank yesterday and found out where Matt was staying.

Chapter 22

It was a good thing Page hadn't gotten herself in some kind of trouble while he'd been sick. But the important thing was that they'd found each other—no more frantic, frustrated searching. If they landed into any more adventures now, they'd at least be in them together.

Matt ran down the stairs to the lobby, enduring the pain, because it was faster and he was late. But when he trotted into the hotel dining room and saw her sitting at a table by herself, when she looked up and scowled at him, what he felt was relief. A part of him must've been worried she'd disappeared again, and he was delighted to lock eyes on her. Their eyes met, and he grinned.

He walked over to the table, shaking his head as he looked at the delicate china tea set and the silver tray and the multi-level platter with its vast assortment of cookies and cake slices. She hadn't waited for him to order.

As he took his seat across from her, she gave up glaring and started pouring him a cup of tea. He'd have preferred a mug of coffee, but he didn't think it was a good time to make an issue of that. He'd just enjoy the tea, watered down as it was with milk.

He looked her in the eye again as she passed the saucer and cup over. "You would not believe what I went through looking for you." Why hadn't she just waited for him in San Francisco?

Page gave him a blank look. "You'll have to tell me all about it. Some other time." And she took one of the slices of cake onto a little plate and cut it with her fork. "Right now we're supposed to be enjoying morning tea." And she stuffed that bite of cake into her mouth.

Matt shook his head. "Looks more like dessert to me, but I suppose you got them to do all this anyway." She had her fixed ideas about history, how it should be—like being courted by gentlemen in fancy dress who swept women off their feet with ballroom dancing. It might have been like that, but Matt preferred the more casual and real present that he was used to.

At that moment, a tall man in an exquisitely tailored navy blue suit came and stood over their table —with thick, slicked-back hair and a tiny little mustache, he looked like a lothario. The smooth operator ignored Matt and concentrated on Page, glaring at her with narrowed eyes.

"I believe we had a date to go dancing yesterday evening. Not only did you stand me up, but I understand you've been shamelessly cavorting with some strange man. You were correct to name yourself an adventuress—you're no better than you should be."

Page frowned up at him as she chewed her cake and washed it down with a gulp of tea. "You're mistaken. We didn't have any date."

Chapter 22

Matt was glad she was reacting so calmly to the man's attitude, but he wasn't going to stand for her being insulted in that snide manner. He caught her eye and asked, "Has this guy been bugging you?"

She nodded slightly. "He seems to be under the delusion that I'm enamored of him, or that I would be, given half the chance. But I've been too busy to consider how best to disillusion him. Circumstances, though, seem to have done that for me."

Standing up out of his chair, Matt automatically began to growl, but his throat was still sore. "I know you can take care of yourself, Page, but I would love to defend your honor."

The man drew himself up to his full height, then turned his attention to Matt. "I would answer your challenge with a duel, if you dared."

"With swords, or do you mean pistols at dawn?" Matt shook his head. "I'd rather just beat you to a pulp right now for besmirching her honor."

"I am Henry Riggleston, the Second. You would not dare lay hands on me."

Page cut another hunk of cake with her fork and looked at Matt. "Alright, go ahead and thrash him within an inch of his life, if that will satisfy your conception of chivalry. But do you mind if I keep eating while I watch?"

Riggleston sputtered and his lower lip quivered as he spoke. "If you lay even one finger on me, I will see you thrown in jail—into the deepest dungeon for the rest of your life. I have powerful friends in positions of influence in this city."

Matt grinned. "I do believe it would be worth it to give you a good pummeling. The police just took the cuffs off and let me loose a couple days ago, you know. My wrists are still chafed. Even so—"

"You're insane. I'm going to see someone now, and I'll make sure they arrest you if you stay in New York." Saying that, he backed away from the table, turned, and almost ran out of the dining room.

Looking at all those cookies and cakes still to be enjoyed, Matt shook his head and looked at Page. "I think we'd better eat up—they'll probably come toss us out of the hotel soon."

Page washed down her last bite of cake and took a couple cookies. "They may throw you out—acting that way. But they won't make *me* leave."

"You'd stay here without me?"

"In a heartbeat."

Matt grinned. "Then I guess I'll have to fight all of them off until you're ready to go. But remember, we may have found each other, but we still have no idea what happened to Turner and Verity. Without knowing their frequencies, I can't locate them with the temporal tuner. And if we're headed back to the twenty-first century, we've got a long way to go, and we can only Travel safely three years at a time."

Chapter 22

Page nodded. "It may take a while, so there's no rush. And I don't just mean for finishing our tea. I came back to your time to study twentieth-century dating customs, and here we are, right at the beginning. Or close to, anyway. So I want to take the opportunity to do some proper research."

"What about Turner and Verity?"

"We can keep an eye out for them, and for Sam and Bailey, as we work our way slowly back toward two thousand twelve. If that's how far we have to go to find everyone. But since we're all time-travelers, why should it matter how long we take?"

He thought it might matter a lot. They each existed in their own separate but relative timestreams, which should mean a month for them would also be a month for Turner and Verity. If they took a whole year to get back—but he'd spent three years on the slow path from nineteen twelve to nineteen fifteen, and it clearly hadn't been three years to Page.

But he couldn't tell her that. "You're right. We should take our time and see the sights. I'd like taking in some history, and we wouldn't want you rushing your research."

Page paused with a cookie halfway to her mouth and smiled. "We'll start now. I haven't even withdrawn any of this year's stipend yet, nor had time to do any proper shopping. And you shouldn't worry about Riggleston."

"Alright, I won't. You know, in just a couple of weeks now they'll be signing the Armistice. And all that fighting will stop, and everyone will be coming home, and there'll be a lot of celebrating going on. It would be a shame to miss that."

"Indeed. I understand the tango is popular, and that will give us two weeks to learn it."

Matt gulped. He was still recovering, and from what he understood, the tango was rather demanding. "I'm looking forward to the twenties. Prohibition and speakeasies, gangsters and Tammany Hall, flappers and the foxtrot."

"Is that what the twenties are really like?"

Matt finally took a cookie for himself. "I'm not sure, but I guess we'll find out."

Chapter 23
Nye at the Ngaio

August 15th, 2003 Midtown Manhattan

NYE started at the sound of a knock on the door. It was an unwanted interruption, just when she'd settled down to review the day's research, and an unusual one. The only people who ever visited her suite were her fellow Travelers—but Anya should be safely out of the way, back in Chickadee with Tate, and the others had all gone to two thousand twelve. *Perhaps it's one of the maids?*

When she had climbed out from the cushions of the large armchair she'd ensconced herself in, then trotted over to the door to glance through the peephole, though, what she saw was Special Agent Coulter and at least a couple other FBI men with him.

Nye knew she would have to open the door. The hotel manager or one of the maids would open it for them, if they didn't just break it down. She couldn't understand why they'd come for her again, though. The other times she had been out doing something, only for her actions to have been misinterpreted by the authorities—but she'd been sitting quietly in her own rooms this evening. Eating, writing, and starting her review. Nothing that federal agents should even know about, much less be able to misconstrue. *So why are they here?*

She pushed the bridge of her glasses to start recording, then with a sigh she unlocked the deadbolt, opened the door, and stared at the familiar face. She would have to rely on her intelligence, and her lawyer if necessary, to protect her from the FBI. *I managed to handle them twice before.*

Agent Coulter was smiling—making an effort to, according to her glasses—and Nye noted that in her file. None of the other agents ever smiled. Why that was could be an interesting study.

Waiting for him to say or do something, Nye acknowledged to herself that this was an opportunity, not only to analyze people's behavior, but maybe to get Kirin's watch out of the FBI's possession. She'd need to look around when they dragged her down to the New York field office this time. If she was going to get that Travel device back, she needed to acquire

Chapter 23

a lot of specific information about that place and the way they operated at the FBI. The silence continued for a long, protracted moment, but Nye was content to wait as long as she had to.

Agent Coulter was not. "Miss Walker. My apologies for disturbing you like this, but I'm hoping for your help with something. May we come in?"

Nye stood back from the door. "Of course." She turned and led the men into the sitting room. "But I must say this is different from how you've asked for my help before." And it gave her no opportunity to gather more data on their offices—she would have to keep analyzing the video she'd already gotten.

One of the agents positioned himself in the entryway near the door, while the other carried a black case to her desk and set it on the clean surface, then perched himself on a chair. Agent Coulter took the armchair opposite the one Nye had been sitting in— he must've noticed the depressed cushions. She sat down on the edge of that chair and waited, again.

"You were helpful the other two times I needed to ask you questions, so I thought we might as well be comfortable this time." He smiled at her, again. "You do want to help, don't you?"

Nye squinted at him. "I'm not sure I do." Maybe they'd relent and drag her in. "You never did tell me what you were investigating at the soup kitchen, besides me."

Agent Coulter's smile didn't falter. "It's not my habit to share that kind of information with outsiders. But in this instance it may be necessary, relevant even, to what I want your help with."

"Well, I'm waiting."

"We'd been hearing increased chatter about the possibility terrorists might try to recruit a homeless person to help with an upcoming attack. So we began watching places where that might occur."

Nye shook her head. "Chatter is nothing but the aggregation of intimations from signal intelligence. I doubt your methodology could be sound enough to produce reliable results. At least hard signal intelligence is useful."

He paused to look around the room. "You may not have heard of the incident outside the UN building this afternoon—a small bomb went off. Thankfully no one was injured."

"No, I hadn't heard." He must've noted the lack of a television. "But it would explain those three fire trucks I saw speeding in that direction four minutes before three."

He nodded to himself. "This is in strictest confidence, you understand?" At her nod, he turned and nodded to the agent sitting at her desk, who opened his case and removed a laptop.

Agent Coulter continued. "This time no one got hurt, and we don't want there to be a next time, and

Chapter 23

we think you might be able to help us stop that, you and your memory. Naturally, we're trying anything we can think of to track down the perpetrator. That includes coming to you."

Nye nodded. "Anyone who'd set off a bomb and got away with it would be likely to do it again. You'd want to find him as fast as possible to prevent a recurrence. One that might be more destructive. Of course I'll help, if I can."

"You've spent a lot of time at that soup kitchen, and around the Kips Bay area, which is not far from the UN Headquarters. We've got surveillance video of the man who planted the bomb, but it's not clear enough for running facial recognition—your memory might be able to tell us something though."

The other agent had booted up his laptop, and he brought it over to sit on the arm of her chair and play the video Agent Coulter had referred to. It was a grainy, low-resolution recording, and it showed a man leaving a backpack on the ground, leaning it up against one of the large waste receptacles. The way he was dressed was similar to the people Nye knew who lived on the street. The agent hit a button, and the screen was filled with a freeze-frame image, the best there was of the bomber.

"It looks as if that 'chatter' of yours was correct this time, but that doesn't validate the practice. And I can't see his face clearly enough to tell you when or where I'd seen him before, or even if. I'm sorry, but I don't know what you expected of me."

Agent Coulter shook his head. "We're still looking for other, clearer footage of the man, but I don't hold out much hope. But our software can only examine faces, while you can recall everything you've seen. Take a good look at the clothes he's wearing, the shape of his body. Any detail might identify him for you, in a way it wouldn't for us. Even if you don't know *who* he is, if you've seen him before, anything you remember of him could be helpful."

Nye blinked to start running an analysis, comparing the video of the man placing the backpack to all of her recorded images. Even her advanced software could not recognize that blurry face, but Agent Coulter was correct that *she* did not have to depend on faces alone.

While her program was running, she talked. "I *have* noticed that most homeless people keep wearing the same clothes, and often have quite a distinctive appearance, one from another. I may be able to help."

It took over a minute for the search subroutine to come up with its results and display them on her lenses. It showed only one instance of the same silhouette, and she watched the footage twice.

Then she brought up the associated data points and looked at Agent Coulter. "I did see the man be-

Chapter 23

fore, once. On the seventh of August at ten twelve in the morning, that man was shuffling along the sidewalk in Times Square, heading south. He stopped at a trash can and briefly searched the top layer of deposits in a most haphazard manner, then proceeded on his way. That's all I saw."

"You didn't see him going in or out of any building? Or talking to anyone? Did you get a good look at his face? We might be able to put a sketch of the man together."

Nye held her hand up in the air to stop him talking to her—it was a distraction. "Yes, I can see the man's face quite clearly." Her glasses recorded everything in high resolution, unlike those useless surveillance cameras.

"Great. Agent Thompson has advanced identification software on his laptop that can help us generate a sketch right now. With your help."

Nodding absently, Nye was working on another task she hoped would be even more helpful. Isolating the man's face from the better quality video she had of him, she then ran those features through the search program against all the faces she'd recorded. Then she turned to look at Agent Thompson and his laptop. He was actually smiling at her.

She noted that fact for her file on the FBI as she listened to him explaining what he wanted her to do to help him assemble a sketch starting with a small selection of different facial features. All she was required to do was choose the hair, the chin, the ears, the nose, and so forth, that most closely resembled the man whose face she was seeing reflected on her lenses. Then he took her through each feature once again, with less variegated selections from which to choose. It was quite simple, and in little time Agent Thompson had finished his sketch. It moved much slower than her glasses, though, which had finished her search request long before.

The young agent was almost gleeful. "And you *are* sure this looks like him?"

Nye snorted. She ran an analysis of that sketch he'd produced, against her own high-quality image, and found it an easy match. "It's quite a good likeness. I'd say about ninety-two percent on common points of comparison." Her glasses said ninety-two point seven. "It should be sufficient to run through your facial recognition software."

Agent Thompson looked to his boss for permission, and Coulter nodded. "Go ahead and connect to our database and run the image like a photo." Then Special Agent Coulter looked at Nye and gave what her glasses described as a genuine smile. "I have to thank you, Miss Walker. I think you've been a real help to us."

"Wait, there's more. I told you I can see his face clearly from that time in Times Square. I reviewed

Chapter 23

all the other faces I've seen recently, and I had seen the same man on one other occasion."

"And you're just now recalling this?"

Nye nodded. "Yes. The first time I was trying to recall someone wearing those clothes. I tried again once I could see his face—I found I'd seen that same man before, but wearing different clothes."

His face froze, and his skin seemed to bristle as if his hairs were standing up, but Nye's kinesis program didn't show any physical alteration in his posture. After a short pause, he asked her the obvious question. "And what clothes was he wearing then?"

"He wore a slate-gray suit, a silk tie with a purple and white pattern, and black dress shoes. Some sort of cufflinks also, but I was too far away to make out any detail." Even her high-resolution video had its limits. She went on to answer the other, implied questions. "It was the Garment District on the first of August—he was entering a warehouse on Thirty-seventh Street at twenty-one minutes past eleven in the morning. He didn't look homeless, then."

Agent Coulter stared at her for a moment. "No, indeed." Then he glanced at his subordinate. "Did you get that, Thompson?"

"Yes, sir. Of course, sir."

"Good. Now, why don't we have you show Miss Walker some of the photos we have of known terror suspects to see if she recognizes the man?"

He looked back at Nye. "You don't mind taking the time to help us out a little more, do you?"

"Of course not. But I don't think such a laborious undertaking is necessary."

He ignored her and took out a cell phone. A few seconds later he was asking someone to get him the details of the warehouse at the address she had given him. When he finished giving out instructions to people over the phone, he turned back to her. "Now I'll leave Thompson here with you—"

The young agent was so excited he interrupted his boss, shoving the laptop in Agent Coulter's face as he spoke. "We already got a hit off facial recognition. And look who it is."

Coulter gave Thompson a momentary glare before looking at the laptop. He blinked. "We didn't even know he was in the country."

Nye piped up to ask. "Who is he?"

He squinted at her for a second. "I don't imagine his name would mean anything to you, but he's known to us. So your assistance has been far more helpful than I'd dared hope."

"You're welcome."

"You are quite extraordinary, you know. I hope you realize that."

"I'm not, really." It was her glasses. "But if you can come back some other time, to show me photos of terrorists, then I'd know if I ran into them."

Chapter 23

Agent Coulter had turned and started to leave—that brought him back to stare at her. "That would be a good idea. You spend a lot of time walking the streets of Manhattan, Miss Walker. You might just happen to see something, and it would be worth the effort to show you those photos. Maybe I should see about hiring you as a consultant. You'd have to pass a background check of course."

Nye cocked her head at him. "Considering how thoroughly you've already researched me, wouldn't that be redundant?"

"We're often redundant, but we're thorough. So we don't make many mistakes."

A warning signal sounded in her head. Getting hired as a consultant for the FBI would afford her a lot of opportunities to accomplish different goals. It would also give *them* the potential of learning more about her. But, on balance, she thought it would be worth the risk.

Chapter 24
Expecting

June 1st, 2013 Chickadee County

VERITY leaned on the railing and levered herself, step by step, onto the porch and waddled across the wooden planks to unlock the front door. Maybe she was being paranoid, but she'd been staying here two weeks, and every time she had taken a walk outside, she had locked the door behind her. Out here in the middle of nowhere. Hollingsworth had brought her up here himself and given her a key to the property. He'd approved of her coming up here to wait in the hope of finding her husband, or one of the others at least—someone who knew where she'd find Turner. Or could track him down, if that possibility even existed.

Chapter 24

Unless things had changed, the Travelers would have left at the end of the previous summer, passing over the past nine months Verity had been slogging through, and could soon be landing here at the start of a new summer. As far as she was aware, they did not set any regular date, but could show up any time vaguely identifiable as early summer. So Verity had taken her maternity leave in the middle of May and come up here to camp out in the Travelers' house—waiting and hoping. It would be nice if her husband showed up before the baby.

A spasm shook her, and she grabbed at the door frame as she was stepping inside. Her first contraction, but she wasn't going to panic. Even if this was really the beginning of labor, she would have plenty of time to call Ralph for a ride, or an ambulance if it was an emergency. And she understood labor could last a long time—or a *very* long time. She also knew that contractions didn't necessarily mean going into labor right now, or at all, and her due date was still a few days away.

Then she heard the sound of a car coming down the lane and wondered if it was just a coincidence or if someone could have known that she might need a ride soon. She stared as a big black SUV came into view—not Ralph. She considered closing and locking the door. And wondered whether she should do that from the inside or the outside.

Mr. Hollingsworth would've called first, and arrived in his luxury sedan—or hers, since he'd insisted on holding on to it until Verity returned to work. She tried to think who else it might be. It certainly wouldn't be Anya and the others turning up by such conventional means.

She hesitated too long—by the time the inviting coolness from the air-conditioning in the house had made her decision for her, the SUV with tinted windows had stopped in front of the porch, and its door was already opening. She was surprised to see little Nye, of all people, climbing down out of the driver's seat. Then again, at least a couple of years must've gone by from Nye's perspective, more than enough time for her to learn how to drive.

The girl came and stood at the foot of the porch and stared up at Verity with a keen, unnerving scrutiny. Nye glanced across to the barn and then down at her watch before ascending to the porch. "Where did you come from?"

Was she comparing my size to the barn? Verity smiled. *Or is that strange look she's giving because I've been missing.* Some things hadn't changed, like Nye's manners. "That's the question I was going to ask you. Shouldn't you be popping out of thin air?"

"You didn't answer my question."

With a grin she complied. "I've been right here, waiting for you, or rather for any of you, for the past

Chapter 24

two weeks. Prior to that, I came from Mr. Hollingsworth. Your lawyer."

The girl cocked her head. "Hollingsworth? But you and Page and Matt and Turner all left from two thousand two. You were supposed to show up here a year ago. What happened to you? Where are the rest? Matt and Page?"

"Don't forget my husband. I don't have any idea what became of Turner and the others. I only know that I landed on the eighth of September, three full months later than when we were supposed to arrive, and all on my own." Verity clutched the door frame as another contraction came. "If you don't mind, I'd like to go inside and sit down now. We can continue this conversation in more comfortable circumstances, can't we?" Although it was more like an interrogation than a chat.

Nye nodded, following Verity inside and talking to her back as she waddled into the living room. "I think they must've just missed you. Anya and Tate, they left on the evening of the eighth."

Verity eased herself onto the couch. "I must've missed them by hours, if not minutes. But what are you doing here instead of there, with them wherever they are?"

"They're nowhere. In the past, in the future. As for me, I've got too much work to do to be skipping nine months out of the year. I'm on the slow path."

A grunt escaped from Verity. "Like me. You've been here, somewhere, all along. While I have been waiting nine months to find one of you."

Nye took a seat across the coffee table from her and leaned forward with a piercing stare. "Mr. Hollingsworth didn't tell you I was around?"

"He knew? He didn't say a word to me."

The girl nodded to herself and leaned back, but she still seemed intent on Verity. "When the four of you didn't materialize three months ago, Anya knew something had gone wrong, but obviously you can't tell us anything about what that was. Matt or Page should be able to shed some light on it, if they ever turn up."

Verity wondered if the girl was trying to be considerate, not to mention Turner, or was she jealous? "I hope Anya, at least, shows up soon. I have something to give her. And not only that—" Another contraction cut off her words. The pain was worse this time, and she started her breathing to help with it.

"Not only what?"

Clenching her teeth until the pain subsided, she thought that Nye hadn't changed as much as it had first appeared. "Which do you want to know about, the watch someone sent to Hollingsworth, or how I am probably in labor and could be ready to deliver this baby before long?" And none too soon—even if Nye was the only one there to help.

Chapter 24

Nye squinted at her through her glasses. "If you just started having contractions, we should have the time to discuss the other matter first. And it might help distract you from the pain. Now, what about a watch?"

Verity grabbed her purse and took out the Travel device, holding it up for the girl to peer at. "Some secret admirer of Hollingsworth's sent him this. In the mail." Along with something more important in her opinion.

"When did it arrive, exactly?"

"About three months ago. Look, it's an interesting story, but—"

This time it was Nye who cut her off rather than another contraction. *It's preferable to the pain.*

"I need to know the day that Mr. Hollingsworth received that watch. I'm sure you can recall the date if you try."

Verity glared at the girl, but she wasn't about to resist the challenge. Even with everything going on it only took her a minute to remember the details—and Nye carefully extracted them all. Everything to do with how it was packaged and sent, to the critical video of a murder on a USB drive, Verity described for the girl—even the file format used and the brand of the memory stick.

Nye reached out to take the watch and examine the back before returning it to Verity. "You probably should keep that. Give it to Anya or not, it's your decision."

Verity found herself rolling her eyes. "Alright—but right now I need to go and freshen up, and then call the hospital to see if they want me to come in."

She pushed until she finally escaped the pull of the sofa and got to her feet. She started toward the hall and the half bath, but another contraction came halfway across the living room, and she reached out and clung to an end table to keep from falling. Then her water broke. *It's happening too fast.* The hardwood floor in the living room would at least make it easy to clean up. She was just getting over the pain when a new wave hit, almost before she'd been able to catch her breath. As it began to subside, she tried to grin at Nye.

"I think going to the hospital is definitely called for. Unless *you* know how to deliver a baby."

"I have the information, but I doubt it would be a good idea for me to try to perform a delivery."

Gritting her teeth in a semblance of a smile, she could only be glad of that. "I think I'm the one who will actually be doing the work, but if you could help me sit back down and then call for a ride to the hospital, I'd be grateful."

"Well, if you really feel you need to go, I'll drive you there. But shouldn't you be able to do this all on your own—otherwise why are you out here by your-

Chapter 24

self? I can see you already know all those breathing techniques."

Verity had a hard time not shouting at Nye. "I'd come hoping my husband might be here. He ought to be here for this." She clenched her teeth again as another contraction made her want to howl. "As for doing it on my own—when you're having a baby you can try that yourself. I want a doctor."

"Would a nurse do?"

A wave of relief swept over her when she heard Anya's voice calling from the foyer. Then the woman herself appeared at the living room door. Verity let loose a long sigh. "You'll certainly be a lot more help than Nye's being." She saw Tate hanging back in the hallway.

Anya charged into the room and grabbed Verity by the arm. "Help me get her propped up on the sofa, Nye." The two women helped her get back to the couch, and Anya stuffed pillows behind her so she'd be half-sitting and half-lying down. But she did not need to be made comfy, she needed the pain to stop.

Verity moaned as another contraction hit, gritting her teeth against the pain. She did her breathing until she could talk again. "It just keeps getting worse."

"Well, yes. And the worst is yet to come." Anya turned to Nye. "How far apart are the contractions coming?"

Nye blinked. "The second one was four minutes and sixteen seconds after the first, going by the gritting of her teeth. But they've been coming closer to each other. After we finished talking they were less than two minutes apart. It's hard to tell now."

Anya gave Verity a gentle smile. "Do you mind if I take a look to see how you're coming along?"

"Please do. I'm so glad you showed up. I think Nye wanted to drive me into the hospital instead of calling an ambulance." Verity relaxed and sank into the cushions with a sigh.

"Well. Hopefully there won't be any need to go to the hospital at all, but if there is, she can drive us there. But now isn't the time to try moving you if we don't have to. You're almost fully dilated. Soon you should start feeling the urge to push. Don't fight it, just do your breathing and go with that feeling."

"I'm glad *you* know what you're doing." Verity turned her head to glare at Nye. "You can take that as an official comment on your attitude, if you like."

Both women ignored her, and Anya looked over her shoulder at Tate who was hovering in the background. "Boil some water and bring me some clean towels. When the water's boiling, sterilize a couple of clothespins and a sharp pair of scissors."

Tate took off, and Verity stared intently at Anya to make sure she had the woman's attention. "You really are going to deliver my child here and now?"

Chapter 24

"It's all really quite straightforward, you know. And it may have been a while, but I've had plenty of experience. It's like riding a bicycle. But if anything does go wrong, we'll race you to the hospital, where I'm sure they'd be able to take care of you."

A surge of pain came with the next contraction, and, when Verity could catch her breath again, she made herself smile back at Anya. "Thank you. And later, would you remind me that if I never see Turner again it will be too soon."

"Now, now. You'll feel differently about that before long. Have you decided on a name for the baby yet?"

"A name? I never let them tell me if it would be a boy or a girl. And I've been too busy to do a lot of research on names."

Nye piped up from somewhere behind her. "I'd be able to help you with that at least. Are there any criteria I can use to narrow down the results?"

"Like what?"

Anya shook her head. "Surely you've given the matter *some* thought?"

"In idle moments, maybe. But I'm not interested in naming the baby after anyone in my own family, and I don't know anything about Turner's. Note that I don't care about his opinion right now—but I don't even know his real last name. There are a few people who've been so kind to me that—"

She cut herself off as a new contraction brought more pain, and she started huffing and puffing with abandon. "I'm going to have to push now."

"Then you go right ahead, and don't try to talk. Just push. Though I should warn you, I think—"

Burning, searing pain tore through Verity's entire body, and her eyes flooded with tears—and the pain just kept coming.

"—I can already see the baby's head." Anya had to raise her voice over the sound of Verity's screaming. "You're crowning. The absolute worst pain has almost arrived, when the baby's shoulders come out—but that's the last of it. And then you'll be able to relax."

Verity felt hysterical laughter begin bubbling up within her. The pain couldn't get any worse, or she wouldn't be held responsible for the consequences.

Epilogue
A New Life

June 1st, 2013 Chickadee County

ANYA grinned from ear to ear as she held the baby in the kitchen sink, carefully cleaning the blood and amniotic fluid off with a gentle stream of water. To her, the child—raw, scrawny and pink, with a mat of straw-colored hair plastered to its head—was magnificent. She felt a warm overflowing joy within her just to be holding the baby—she'd forgotten the intense satisfaction of helping with a delivery, so long ago had it been. Too long.

Nye came in carrying a pail and wearing rubber gloves. "I took care of the placenta, and cleaned up as best I could, but I think we'll need a new sofa."

"And how's Verity doing?"

Nye shrugged. "She's resting. But she says she won't sleep until she sees the kid again." Nye took a close look at the baby. "I'm not sure why she wants to."

Anya sighed. "Naturally she desires to hold her child in her arms. She went through a lot bringing this baby into the world, and she deserves that."

To her side, Tate held a towel out, ready to dry the infant off. When she'd finished washing it, she lifted the baby out of the sink and into the enfolding towel. While Tate dried, Anya took a soft blanket in her hands, then received the baby back, wrapping it up with gentle precision. And she stood there, staring into its adorable scrunchie face until Tate began coughing to get her attention.

"Yes, we need to take the child to its mother."

Tate followed her back into the living room. "I haven't seen you look this happy in a long time, Anya."

"Because it's been a while since I've felt so good about what I was doing." Nine summers she'd been doing her research with Tate and trying to forget all the mess she'd made trying to save the professor. It wasn't enough, even with fiddling in the garden and learning to do a few small repairs, to make some improvements to the house. Her days had been filled, but not with joy. But she was experiencing that deep happiness and contentment now.

Epilogue

Anya walked over to the couch, where Verity lay looking exhausted and peaceful, ragged and radiant all at the same time. She placed the swaddled infant into the new mother's arms to cradle. "There you go —a beautiful baby girl. Now, you will have to name her before long. It's important."

Verity beamed as she stared into the little girl's eyes. "Olivia. I don't know why, but her name needs to be Olivia. It's just right. Olivia Silver Belue."

"Olivia is a good name. The rest doesn't matter but that's a good name for the child. Now, I'll let the two of you have some time together, for mother and daughter to bond. But then you'll need to get some sleep."

The woman might as well not have heard, for all her attention was on the infant. Anya stepped back and gave them room, but continued to watch them. It was an amazing thing to see.

Finally she tore her eyes away, and went to join Tate and Nye who were standing in the hall just outside. "I need to talk to you both. I've made my decision."

She looked first at Tate. "We're going to be taking the slow path from now on. Like Nye." Who was now ten years older than in two thousand three, but Anya had only gained a little over two years during that same interval. Nye was catching up with her. "I hope you're alright with that."

Tate smiled. "Of course, Leader. Anything that you want us to do, it's alright with me."

Anya sighed and turned to Nye. "Since I'm not going to be Traveling, you might as well take care of this." Unstrapping the leader device from her wrist, she handed it over to the girl. "You've shown you're responsible, so you can take responsibility for that—I'll be too busy."

Nye cocked her head. "As if I won't be?"

Anya shook her head. "Tate and I will be helping Verity take care of the baby." She turned to him and continued. "In addition to that, and all our research, I want to go back to nursing. It's been quite a while since I practiced, and their medicine is very different anyway, and since I don't have any credentials here—I'll have to go to nursing school first."

It was a very good thing that there had been no complications with Verity's delivery. It had all gone smoothly—the baby had come out head first and begun wailing all on its own. Then Anya had clamped and cut the umbilical cord, and now mother and infant were doing fine.

If anything had gone wrong, they could've taken Verity to the hospital. But Anya didn't like knowing she would have been unprepared to deal with whatever problems might've come up.

Tate nodded slowly. "That will be a lot of work to take on, and it will mean having a lot more direct

Epilogue

contact with the contemporaries. More questions to answer about who we are and where we came from. And—" He paused and gave her a kind look. "What you'll experience as a nurse won't all be as joyful as this."

"Yes, I know, and you're sweet to think of that, but I did alright volunteering after 9/11. The things I had seen before that—it's all way in the past." Her own personal past, but far in the future. "I'm strong enough to face the heartache again now. But I need to do what I can to help people.

"As for becoming more involved with the community, I want to know these people better. We've been holding back a long time, but now. Now we're going to go native, as the professor would say. And as for their questions—we'll just become the backgrounds Page created for us."

Tate kept nodding until she stopped. "And your plan for taking us slowly closer to home by skipping nine months out of every year?"

"Was never going to get us there. It's too far—we'll just have to rely on Matt and Page being able to fix the professor's device, if we want to be able to all go home some day." Of course, that would be most difficult for Tate, who of all of them had the most to go back for.

Nye, who'd been listening in silence, snorted. "I wouldn't get my hopes up about that. Their test trip was a complete disaster. They're likely a whole century away, if not a millennium."

Anya nodded. "It might be, but there's nothing we can do about that. We'll have enough work to do without worrying about things beyond what we can do right now." At least they had the resources to do right by little Olivia. She might not be able to help Turner, wherever and whenever he was, but his little girl was in good hands.

"Speaking of which, I need to go take that baby, so Verity can get the sleep she needs." And it would give her more time with the child. For the first time in a long while, Anya was actually looking forward to the future. With a new life.

About the Author

JAMES LITHERLAND is a graduate of the University of South Florida who currently resides as a Virtual Hermit in the wilds of West Tennessee.

He's lived in various places and done a number of jobs—he has been an office worker and done hard manual labor, worked (briefly) in the retail and service sectors, and he's been an instructor. Through all that, he's always been a writer.

He is a Christian who tries to walk the walk (and not talk much.)

Made in the USA
Charleston, SC
22 July 2016